Grass Grows in the Pyrenees

Grass Grows in the Pyrenees

Elly Grant

Books by the Author

Death in the Pyrenees series:

- Palm Trees in the Pyrenees
- Grass Grows in the Pyrenees
- Red Light in the Pyrenees
- Dead End in the Pyrenees
- Deadly Degrees in the Pyrenees

Angela Murphy series:

- The Unravelling of Thomas Malone
- The Coming of the Lord

Also by Elly Grant

- Never Ever Leave Me
- Death at Presley Park
- But Billy Can't Fly
- Twists and Turns

Chapter 1

For a moment he flew horizontally as if launched like a paper aeroplane from the mountain top, then an elegant swan dive carried him over the craggy stone face of the mountainside. There was no thrashing of limbs or clawing at air; he fell silently and gracefully until a sickening crack echoed through the valley as bone and flesh crunched and crumpled on a rocky outcrop. The impact bounced him into the air and flipped him in a perfect somersault, knocking the shoes from his feet. Then he continued his descent until he came into contact with the grassy slope near the bottom of the mountain, where he skidded and rolled before coming to a halt against a rock.

His body lay on its back, in an untidy heap with arms and legs and shoulders and hips smashed and broken. The bones stuck out at impossible angles and blood pooled around him. He lay like that for almost three days. During that time, the vultures had a feast. There are several species of these birds in the mountains of the Pyrenees and all had their fill of him. Rodents and insects had also taken their toll on the body and, by the time he was discovered, he was unrecognisable.

A hunter found him while walking with his dog and, although he was used to seeing death, the sight of this man's ravaged face, with black holes where his eyes should have been, made him vomit.

Jean-Luc still wore the suit that he'd carefully dressed in for his meeting three days before. It looked incongruous on him in his present condition and in these surroundings. His wallet was still in his pocket and his wedding ring was still on his finger, nothing had been stolen.

The alarm had been raised by his business partner when he failed to turn up for their meeting, but of course, no one had searched for him in this place. This valley was outside of town and on the other side of the mountain from where he'd lived. He wasn't meant to be anywhere near to this place.

His wife hadn't been overly concerned when he didn't return, because he often went on drinking binges with his cronies and he'd disappeared for several days on other occasions. She was just pleased if he eventually came home sober, because he had a foul temper and he was a very nasty drunk. Indeed, she knew how to make herself scarce when he was drunk, as more often than not, she would feel the impact of a well-aimed punch or a kick. Drunk or sober, he lashed out with deadly accuracy and he was quick on his feet.

When he was finally discovered all the emergency services were called into action. The *pompiers*, who were both firemen and trained paramedics, the police and the doctor, all arrived at the scene and an ambulance was summoned to remove the body to the morgue.

Everyone assumed he'd died as a result of his rapid descent from the mountain top and the subsequent impact on the ground below. But what they all wanted to know, was whether his death was a tragic accident, or suicide, or perhaps something darker and more sinister, and why was he in this place, so far from his home or from town? Many questions had to be answered and, being the most senior police officer in this area, meant that I was the person who'd be asking the questions.

Chapter 2

Forgive me, but I seem to have started my story in the middle, so I'll begin again. My name is Danielle and I am the senior police officer in charge of this valley. My jurisdiction is a small town in the French Pyrenees, together with all the surrounding villages, hamlets and farms. I've recently been promoted to this post after many years of being passed over in favour of my male colleagues.

Coincidentally, my promotion has come as a direct result of a previous death by falling. I successfully completed the investigation into that incident, when senior detectives from Perpignan could not. I was praised for my excellent detective work and then offered the opportunity to apply for this higher post with the full backing of my superiors. I passed the examination with flying colours and immediately promoted to my current status. In a short space of time, I have gone from being not much more than a traffic cop, to being the senior policewoman in the area, with responsibility for junior and trainee officers.

The previous incident I mentioned was the demise of a man called Stephen Gold, who fell to his death from the top floor balcony of an apartment block in the centre of town. He was a nasty piece of work and he had no redeeming features. Indeed, most of the people who knew him were happy to see the back of him. Everyone hoped that his Albanian widow would soon also move on. They'd been married for less than a year when he'd died and she inherited a fortune.

Stephen Gold was a business man who managed to make money from everyone and everything. From my investigations, I discovered he was involved in the illegal trafficking of cannabis that has been grown, and is still grown, in the mountains surrounding this town. For years, this type of farming has taken place and the drug has been sold in small quantities throughout the valley. Everybody turned a blind eye to the trade, as it didn't seem to harm anyone and it was never smoked in public or sold to youngsters.

Unfortunately, Monsieur Gold's involvement changed things. He forced each grower to sell him their entire crop, and indeed, to increase their production, which he in turn, trafficked to Eastern European gangsters working in northern Spain. This action made us vulnerable to outside influences and forced the people of the valley into contact with gangs from over the border.

Often I would enter a restaurant only to find a table of strangers sitting with Monsieur Gold. They were always dressed in dark suits, no matter what the temperature. They flashed rolls of banknotes and would never order the *plat de jour*, favouring instead something exotic and expensive from the *a la carte* menu. The patron of the restaurant foisted leftover food on them and charged them a fortune for the privilege. And who could blame him, as they deserved no better. They stuck out like a sore thumb and, had they been tourists instead of gangsters, local people would have made jokes about them. But sensibly, everyone was guarded and wary of them and that was understandable.

They made me feel uncomfortable and I knew that their business was illegal, but I didn't challenge them as common sense told me they were too dangerous. I might be an officer of the law, but I'm not stupid and I don't have a death wish. Instead, I reasoned, that as long as they were plying their trade in Spain and not here, then they could do what they liked. Let the Spanish authorities tackle the problem as it affects their citizens and not mine.

When Stephen died, everyone thought the names of the growers and the locations of their farms died with him and, for a couple of months, everything returned to normal. We had, however, underestimated his widow, Magda.

At first, everybody assumed she would move away. We didn't really care where she moved to, as long as she was gone. However, Stephen had a daughter living in England who contested his will, and that put a hold on the sale of the marital home until a ruling could be made in court. So, much to everyone's disappointment, Magda remained.

During my investigation into Stephen's death, I discovered that prior to being married to him, Magda had been working as a prostitute in northern Spain. I should have realised that she'd become involved in the drug business with her contacts. She was smart enough to figure out the locations of the suppliers, from the information she'd gleaned from her husband before he'd been killed. The business was too lucrative for her to pass up.

Chapter 3

It is the fourteenth of July, Bastille Day. The sun is so strong, I have to wear my sunglasses so I can see to write the parking ticket, which I place under the windscreen wiper of an illegally parked Mercedes. The car has a Spanish registration and looks very expensive. I assume its owner is wealthy and doesn't think our local parking laws apply to him. I can't help smiling at the thought of some spoilt foreigner returning to find my ticket waiting for him.

My town will celebrate Bastille Day with a small parade to pay homage to our military personnel. The parade will be led by the Mayor and accompanied by our local band. It won't be anything like the celebrations in Paris, where the President leads members of the armed forces and visiting dignitaries along the Champs-Elysees in a grand spectacle, but it will be a proud time for all who take part. Our parade will be led by young cadets, followed by armed forces personnel who are home on leave, then finally, any retired old soldiers who live locally.

After the parade there'll be a street party. Restaurant and bar owners will arrange tables and chairs along the main street to supply food and drink for the partygoers. It's a *Fête Nationale*, so all of France will be celebrating today. At nine o'clock tonight the Mayor will lead the revellers to a clearing near the river, then the street lights will be extinguished and we'll be treated to a spectacular fireworks display.

Tomorrow, most of the townspeople will head for the nearby town of Ceret, where there's to be a festival, beginning with the running of the bulls through the streets and followed by much partying and celebrating. There'll be market stalls and *sardane* dancing and, in the bullring on the edge of town, the colourful and exciting spectacle of bull fighting will take place. Bull fights are not to everyone's liking, but in this area of Catalonia, which has both French and Spanish influences, they're a celebrated tradition. The bull fights will be attended not only by locals, but also by many tourists who'll bring money to the area and create a great boost to the local economy.

I'm looking across the road towards the Café, where the patron, his wife and their staff are busy preparing the outside tables for the celebrations, when I become aware of someone standing behind me. They're too close, and I sense my personal space is being invaded.

"I believe this belongs to you," a voice says and I turn to see a tall, muscular man proffering the parking ticket I've just written.

It's thirty degrees in the shade, but this man is wearing a black suit with a shirt and tie. He is immaculately dressed, as are his two companions. He has startling, pale blue eyes that are narrow and piercing and he's very fair-skinned. A long, thin scar runs the length of his face, from his cheek bone to his chin, but it doesn't detract from his fine features. His hair, which at one time was probably naturally blonde, is obviously dyed and has bleached highlights. His colleagues share similar looks. Their jackets seem to bulge around their muscular bodies and I wonder if they're carrying guns. They don't have a hair out of place and are eerily calm and menacing. I'm instantly frightened. I'm hemmed in by them, with my back to the railings which line the pavement at the edge of the road and they're in front, surrounding me. There's no way I can move without pushing my way between them.

"Is there a problem, Monsieur?" I ask. I make myself stand as tall as I can and keep my voice firm, because I think any sign of weakness will have them falling on me like a pack of wild dogs.

"You placed this ticket on my car," he replies, his voice flat and cold. "I like to keep my car very clean, and this ticket makes it look rather untidy." His eyes never leave mine. He's challenging me and his friends are smirking, because they know that I'm intimidated.

"Your car is indeed very clean, Monsieur," I agree, trying to keep my voice from cracking. "But it is also illegally parked. If you do not wish it to be ticketed, then I suggest you park it somewhere else. You have one month to pay the fine."

I've been holding my body taut, but now I exhale slowly and try not to show any fear. He continues to stare at me with his ice-cold eyes then, after a moment, he throws his head back and guffaws with laughter. His friends laugh too.

"Well, officer," he says, "You've certainly put me in my place. Let me introduce myself," he continues, offering me his hand. "My name is Edvard. Perhaps you know my very good friend and business partner, Magda Gold?"

A shockwave runs through my body. His statement confirms that the gangsters have returned to my town. For over two months, nothing has been heard of them, but now they're back. I don't shake his hand. "Excuse me, Monsieur, but I must get on with my work," I say forcefully. I take a deliberate step forward, and the men stand aside to let me pass. In a show of bravado, I add, "Remember that you must pay your fine within one month."

As I walk away, I glance back and see Edvard scrunching up the parking ticket and throwing it into the gutter. I should really turn back and write a second ticket for littering, but I'm not that brave. The reputation of Eddy the Red, as he is referred to, is well known in this valley and only a fool would knowingly upset him, so I pretend I haven't seen what he's done.

Chapter 4

I resist the temptation to look back again, instead making my way over the road to the café. People are beginning to gather for the parade, which is due to start in under half an hour. The two young policemen who've been assigned to assist me today are oblivious to everything that's going on around them, as they're too busy flirting with a group of young, female tourists. They don't even notice me as I pass them by and it's clear, from their body language and their laughter, that they'll be doing little, if any, work today. Finally, when I'm at the door of the café, and safely out of view of the other side of the street, I look back across the road, relieved to see Eddy's car pull away from the kerb and slowly drive off.

There are two men sitting at a table just outside the café entrance. One is tall, thin and wiry, with a Spanish look about him. He has long, straggly hair arranged into two thin plaits which hang on either side of his face. His narrow goatee beard is also plaited, and when he smiles, I can see he has a gold cap on one of his incisors. He's wearing a battered, gaucho-style hat which looks incongruous with his suit. His jacket is slung casually over the chair back and his tie has been loosened, but not removed. I recognise him, his name is Jean-Luc. People call him 'Jean-Luc the Pirate', because he reminds them of Johnny Depp in the film 'Pirates of the Caribbean'.

His companion is a big, thick-set man with distinctively bowed legs. He's almost as wide as he is tall, with a waistline like a roundabout. His complexion is very ruddy, his cheeks are round and his skin shines with perspiration. His bright blue eyes look like large marbles. This man is called Aidan O'Brien and I know that like Jean-Luc, he lives on a farm in the mountains. He is also wearing a suit, but as he's Irish and not French, I know that his formal dress has nothing to do with today's proceedings.

Both of these men are suspected of growing cannabis on their land and I can only assume they've come to town to meet with Eddy the Red. They look furtively at me as I make my way past them. Jean-Luc can't meet my gaze, but Aidan attempts to greet me. "*Bonjour* officer," he says nervously, in a strong Irish brogue. His cheeks are hot and he looks at me for only a moment before dropping his chin and staring at the ground.

"Messieurs," I reply. "What brings you to town today?"

Jean-Luc fires a warning glance at Aidan, who doesn't reply.

"I've brought some of my children to see the celebrations," Jean-Luc says. "Aidan's wife, Siobhan, and their children are also in town, so we thought we'd meet up for a drink."

"And is your wife not in town today?" I ask Jean-Luc. I know that he rarely permits his wife to leave their home, because he won't let her frequently bruised face be seen in public. However, until she makes a complaint about him, he'll continue to hit her and no one will intervene.

"My wife's at home with the two *bébés*. There's a lot of work for her to do, cleaning, cooking and tidying my house. She's much too busy for a day off, and besides, a woman's place is in the home. It's her job to look after me and my children."

"She obviously looks after you very well," Aidan adds with a leer. "That's why you've got five children, Jean-Luc."

Aiden's trying to make me feel uncomfortable and I'm ashamed to say that he's succeeding. They're both laughing and staring at me, challenging me to make a comment. "Enjoy your day, Messieurs," is all I can manage, and as I walk towards the bar, I can hear their laughter ringing in my ears.

I'm happy to see a familiar, friendly face sitting at the bar enjoying a pastis and sharing conversation with the patron. He's a tall, slim English gentleman of about sixty years of age, and as usual, his elegant frame is clothed in fashionable designer wear.

"*Bonjour*, Byron," I say *"Ça va?"*

"Ah, *bonjour Mademoiselle*," he replies, taking my hand in his and kissing it gently. "Perhaps I shouldn't kiss you when you're on duty, but I can't help myself," he says with a wink and a cheeky smile. "And I'm very well. Thank you for asking," he adds. "And you? How are you today?"

"I too am well, thank you," I reply.

I'm very fond of Byron and over the last year or so he's become a good friend to me. Indeed his friendship has been instrumental in my achieving the life I now enjoy.

"I saw you speaking to that motley pair sitting by the door," he continues. "I trust they're up to no good."

"I'm not sure," I reply. "I've just had an encounter with Eddy the Red and I'm wondering if they're involved in business dealings with each other. I'm very upset that gangsters have returned to this town and Eddy's just told me that his business partner is Magda Gold"

"I wouldn't trust any of them as far as I could throw them," Byron replies. "Just be very careful, Danielle. They're a bad lot and I think they could be very dangerous. If things start to kick off, be sure to call for assistance. Don't be too proud to ask for help."

"Don't worry, Byron," I reply. "I'll know if I'm out of my depth."

The truth is, I'd never ask for help, because it's taken me too long to prove myself in this job, so come what may, I'll try to cope with whatever happens.

Chapter 5

All the people who are taking part in the parade have now assembled and the Mayor is glancing nervously at his watch. He is a stickler for being on time, which is rather unusual for a local man. In this town we are never particularly precise when it comes to time-keeping, twenty minutes here or there makes no difference. In fact, when making an appointment, foreigners will often ask, 'is that actual time, or French time?'

Everyone is in position and taking up his place. Standing at the front, beside the Mayor, is our oldest soldier, Didier, who is holding the flag. The flag and the flag-pole are made of lightweight materials, so the old soldier who has been given the honour of carrying it can physically manage the task. This isn't a problem for Didier, because although he's ninety-two years of age he's still a strong, robust man. Unfortunately, his mind is not as strong as his body, and, at times, it drifts off to another place and time.

After a couple of minutes, the band starts to play and the parade begins with much encouragement from the crowd. People are throwing confetti and cheering, many are waving small flags and there's a real party atmosphere. No one is very sure if this parade should be joyous or sombre, but as there's to be a street party immediately afterwards, everyone is getting into the party spirit.

Didier is getting more and more excited and he's thrusting the flag upwards with great gusto as he marches. The Mayor has side-stepped slightly and is looking increasingly nervous as he's afraid of being elbowed by the old man. Suddenly, with a great whoop, Didier thrusts the flag upwards then lets it go. Being a powerful man, he has managed to launch it to a great height. There's a moment of confusion and bumping of instruments as the band members, who are immediately behind Didier and the Mayor, reach up to try to catch the flag before the descending pole injures someone. Fortunately, two of the men manage to get a hand to it and it's lowered safely.

"I'll take that back now," Didier says forcefully and he makes a grab for the flag pole.

"Oh no, you won't," says the man who has it in his grasp.

A scuffle breaks out as they wrestle over the flag, and when the Mayor tries to intervene, Didier throws a punch at him. It lands a glancing blow on his shoulder. Before he can throw a second punch, one of the young police officers steps forward and grabs Didier by the arm. I don't know where he's come from because I didn't see him in the crowd, but I am grateful that he's here.

An elderly lady steps forward from the side of the street. She's wearing a wine-coloured suit, which at one time would have been very smart, but now that she's shrunk with age, seems overly big on her. A matching cloche hat is pinned tightly to her hair with hat pins. "What are you doing, Didier, you old fool?" she cries.

Didier stares at the old girl. "Go home, Mother," he says. "Can't you see I'm in the parade?"

"I'm your wife, not your mother, you idiot!" she replies.

He stares at her for a moment, as if trying to recognise her. "I'm the National Amateur Heavyweight Boxing Champion," he states proudly. "Why would I marry an old woman? My wife

Martha is young and beautiful and she's in the crowd watching my victory parade."

With that he begins to call for Martha, and everyone realises his mind has stepped back in time.

A pretty young woman steps forward, explaining that she works at the local care home for the elderly. She kindly offers her assistance.

"Here is my Martha," Didier says, smiling as he takes the young woman's hand.

She gently leads him from the parade and with his wife in tow, they head off towards his home. Watching them, I see Didier has placed his hand on the young woman's bottom. Some of his instincts have not dulled with age, even if his mind has retreated.

The parade resumes and completes the last hundred metres of its journey. Then the band stops playing and a box is placed on the ground for the Mayor to stand on. Everyone is quiet as he delivers his speech. In it, he praises all our servicemen and women and commemorates our war dead. He makes particular reference to the last World War.

The Mayor's father was a brave member of the Resistance during the war, but he was caught and then executed by the Nazis, and the Mayor cannot forgive the German people for this. He delivers a very un-PC speech and warns everyone of the Nazi threat, which he says is still with us. His speech is met by a mixture of shock and horror from the tourists, who cannot believe their ears. However, local people have heard it all before. I'm relieved when he's finished, as the discomfort his speech causes is embarrassing.

Finally, all the formalities are over and I make my way to the pizza restaurant, where the owner has very kindly offered to give me and my junior officers a meal. We are to be seated at a table beside the Commune Committee, and it's considered an honour to be placed beside the esteemed group of men and women who run this town.

Chapter 6

When I arrive with my colleagues, we take our place at the table which has been set up for lunch. I see that the members of the Commune Committee are already seated. I'm disappointed to discover my seat is opposite Madame Gambil's, as she's both an interfering busybody and a close friend of my mother's. I always try to avoid her if I can, and today I've hardly had time to sit down before she starts.

"I was speaking to your mother in church, Danielle," she begins. "She says she doesn't see much of you since you bought that house with your girlfriend. You know, she's not getting any younger and a daughter can be such a comfort to her mother."

In the space of ten seconds this old cow has upset me and, although I shouldn't rise to the bait, I find I cannot help myself. "Firstly, Madame," I begin, "Patricia is not my 'girlfriend'. We have been best friends since infant school as you well know, and although Patricia is a lesbian and she doesn't hide this, I am not. As for my relationship with my mother, I don't think that it is any of your business."

"I'm so sorry if I have upset you, Danielle," she continues with a sugary tone in her voice. "Sometimes it hurts to hear what people are saying about you, especially if there is truth in their words."

"It seems, Madame, that wherever a person goes in this town, gossip will manage to hit them. It doesn't matter whether it is true or not. There will always be someone, such as yourself, who'll discuss other people's business and the more upsetting and personal it is, the more I'm sure you'll enjoy it." I am bristling with anger; how dare she say these things to me? How dare she discuss my personal life, especially in front of my junior colleagues? She purses her lips and I can see she's annoyed at being spoken back to, but she decides not to pursue the conversation any further. Instead, much to my relief, she ignores me and turns to speak to her neighbour.

The best decision I've ever made was to buy a house with my best friend. It's true that I haven't had much contact with my mother recently, and since I've moved out, I never visit my parent's house, but it's as much my mother's choice as mine. I've never gotten along with her as she resents the fact that I survived, when my brother died of meningitis in childhood. She's always blamed God for choosing to take him instead of me.

The house that Patricia and I have bought is situated at the end of a village, across the river from town. It's enough of a distance away from the nosey gossips, but not so far that we can't walk into the centre of town for our jobs. In this town, everyone likes to know your business and like Madame Gambil, will talk about you simply to make conversation.

The food arrives at the table and it's one of my favourite dishes, steaming bowls of couscous topped with succulent pieces of lamb, chicken and spicy Catalan sausages. An assortment of cooked vegetables served in thin gravy accompanies the couscous. Everyone tucks in with enthusiasm and the conversation flows as freely as the wine.

I'm still upset by my altercation with Madame Gambil so I eat in silence, but this doesn't stop me from listening to the conversations of others. It always amazes me when people will openly discuss their minor crimes such as parking or speeding offences, even though I am sitting beside them. I suppose it's because many of these people still see me as little Danielle, the schoolgirl, and not Danielle, the senior police officer. I strain to overhear snippets of one conversation between two gentlemen who are seated at the end of the table, as I'm sure they're talking about seeing Eddy the Red in town. However, my attempts to hear more are rudely interrupted when Madame Gambil directs her questions to me once again. It seems she's not going to give up easily.

"I saw you today, Danielle," she begins. "You were talking to three men in black suits. Am I correct in saying that they are the same criminals who had business dealings with the late Monsieur Gold?"

A hush falls over the table as everybody's attention is suddenly directed to me.

"Yes, I was speaking to three men dressed in black suits," I reply cautiously. "They were illegally parked and I gave them a ticket. I can't comment on whether or not they are criminals, or if they had any business dealings with the late Monsieur Gold. I'm sure you would know more about that than me. You seem to be very well informed about other people's business," I add spitefully.

She folds her arms and purses her thin lips – her face is like thunder. I'm pleased I've riled the old witch.

"Excuse me, Danielle," a voice from across the table says. I look over at the gentleman who has addressed me and see that it's Monsieur Bonet. He's a very striking character with his white hair and carefully waxed moustache. He always wears a bowtie and has a matching handkerchief in the breast pocket of his suit.

"*Oui*, Monsieur," I reply politely.

"Forgive me," he continues. "But you must realise how concerned we'll be if we learn that these men are indeed back in our town. Some parents of high school children think someone is offering drugs to the teenagers. Are you aware of that?"

"No, I wasn't aware that there was a problem with drugs," I reply. "Nothing has been reported to me. But of course, I'll look into it."

He nods at me. He is satisfied with my answer and our conversation is over. Madame Gambil looks at me with a smug smile. How I detest the woman. Still, I'm very concerned by what I've been told. Eddy the Red is an extremely dangerous man and I would rather not have to deal with him. In fact, I'm not so sure that I could deal with him, because he terrifies me. I decide to do nothing and instead wait and see if anything further happens. With a bit of luck, they'll disappear back to Spain.

Chapter 7

It is Thursday morning, market day, and Patricia and I have woken and risen early. We've both arranged to have our day off today, so we can spend the time together. As I come out of the bathroom after having my shower, I hear my friend singing and her melodious voice fills the house. She's planned this day for weeks and it's very significant for her, because today the farmers will be at the market with their crops of apricots and peaches.

When we first bought our house, we experienced such a sense of freedom. Our lives changed so much for the better, as previously, I'd lived with my depressing and dominating mother and Patricia resided in a rented room. We'd spent weeks planning and talking about the things we'd be able do in our new home. Patricia was particularly looking forward to being able to cook for us. She's a marvellous cook, but had little opportunity in the house where she was living.

As I enter the kitchen, the aroma of freshly-made coffee fills my nostrils and a buttered baguette, stuffed with brie, is on the table for our breakfast. We'd purchased a large, ancient, solid, wooden side table when we moved in and it's just as well, as Patricia has it stacked with gleaming, washed, glass jars of every size. She stops singing and grins at me.

"Today's the day," she says happily. "No more shop-bought jam. Now we'll enjoy my produce. I've managed to get some larger jars for bottling fruit and the supermarket had the alcohol for it on offer. All the sugar that I'll need is over there," she says, pointing to several large bags which are stacked on the work top.

We've been collecting jars since we moved in. Indeed, I'm often handed them in the street when I'm on duty, as Patricia has asked everyone we know, to recycle their jars to us.

"So after breakfast we'll be going to the market to haggle?" I ask.

"Absolutely, yes," she says smiling. "The price is very important and I intend to get a bargain. Will you manage to park your car close to the fruit stalls, because the fruit will be too heavy for us to easily carry up the hill?"

"I'll get close," I reply. "Don't worry. But Patricia, how much jam are you planning to make? Are we supplying the whole town?"

She throws her head back and laughs and her blue eyes sparkle. I can see how happy my friend is and I'm delighted.

"No, I'm not supplying the whole town," she replies. "However, I have orders for eighteen jars of jam and three jars of bottled fruit, and by my reckoning, that'll make me at least thirty euros' profit. Perhaps more, if I buy the fruit by the box instead of by the kilo. I plan to always sell some of my produce so that we can have ours for free. You see, the profit that I make will more than cover the cost of our ingredients."

I'm impressed with my friend. She has always wanted to have her own business, and at this rate, she might just manage it. Today is significant, because the peach and apricot crop is the first one to be ready since we moved into our house. Unfortunately, the cherry crop in May was too soon for us to utilise.

We hastily eat our breakfast, although I don't think Patricia managed to swallow much food as she's too excited. It's still only 7.30, but she already has her purse in her hand and she's impatiently pacing the floor waiting for me to be ready.

She chatters on the short journey to the market and I realise, from what she says, that once we return with our purchases, the remainder of the morning and much of the day will be spent preparing fruit. I plan to buy some wine, cold meats, salad and cheese because it doesn't look as if there'll be time to actually cook a meal today. Besides, it's such a glorious, sunny day that the cold food will be a very acceptable alternative.

When we arrive, we see there are four fruit growers at the market and I leave my friend to haggle with them while I go to buy the rest of our produce. I've just purchased two bottles of good local wine when I'm approached by Phillipe, the local vet.

"Bonjour Danielle," he says. "You're early today."

"So are you, Phillipe," I reply.

"I was hoping to see you in your office later," he continues. "Aren't you working? Is this your day off?"

"This is my day off," I reply, "but do you have a problem? Is there something urgent?"

"Not so much urgent as concerning. I've just come from the farm owned by the O'Brien family and most of their animals are dead. The horse and the goat have been shot and the chickens have had their necks wrung. Only the two dogs survived, because they were in the house with the family. Someone has also placed food tainted with rat poison close to the house, presumably meant for the dogs. Madame O'Brien was hysterical when she called me."

"I'm not surprised," I reply. "Who could have done such a thing?"

"I have no idea. I've never heard of such a thing in all my years working as a vet. Madame O'Brien told me that her husband and his associate Jean-Luc were in Spain. When I asked her what they were doing there, she became very guarded. She said they'd simply gone over the border to La Jonquera to buy cheap supplies, but I didn't believe her. I think they're up to no good."

"Did you see anything suspicious?" I question.

"No. Not really. The way they have laid out the farm meant that I could only see a very small area where the animals were kept. Everything else is hidden from view. I believe she only called me because she was frightened and her husband was away. I think that when she got over the shock of finding the dead animals, she was sorry she'd panicked and phoned me. After I arrived, she couldn't get me out of the place quickly enough."

"Should I visit her today?" I ask.

"No, Danielle, enjoy your day off. Today or tomorrow will make no difference to the poor dead creatures. Besides, you might just get the chance to question Monsieur O'Brien if you wait until tomorrow."

I thank Phillipe and wish him a good day, then go to look for my friend. When I do find Patricia, I discover that she's bought fruit from two of the growers. She is waiting for me, with the boxes piled on small barrows to be transported to my car. We place the boxes in the boot and on the back seat and a pungent, fruity aroma fills the car. As we head home from the market, the sun streams through the windows and the sky is a bright, clear blue and I manage to put all thoughts of the O'Brien family out of my mind.

Chapter 8

I arrive at the office early, so I can sort out some work for the two junior officers who've been assigned to me this month. I expect to spend most of the morning travelling to and from the O'Brien's farm and I don't want them to waste their time while I'm away. They're not the most enthusiastic of workers, so if I don't actually give them a task, they'll do nothing.

When I was a young policewoman, I looked for things to do because I wanted my superiors to notice me. Perhaps because I was a woman, performing what was seen to be a man's job and I had to work so much harder than my male colleagues to prove myself. I won't be able to judge if all woman officers work harder than their male counterparts until I am sent a female trainee, but as there are so few of them, that could take years. So for now, I'll just have to keep prodding the lazy young men they send me, if I want to get any work done.

I leave the office as soon as the first trainee arrives and walk to my car. I've checked the route to the O'Brien's farm and I'm relieved to have a four-wheel drive, as their home is near the highest point of a winding mountain road.

As I drive higher and higher into the mountains, I'm amused by the road signs warning of cattle. The tourists must think it impossible for cattle to survive on these rocky crags but suddenly, as you round a corner, there they are, clinging to the small strips of grass at the road side. The large beasts with long horns and bells round their necks are munching happily. I cannot recall any accidents involving these cattle, but I'm sure that some must have occurred in the past or the signs wouldn't be here.

After driving for nearly an hour, I almost miss the entrance to the track leading to the O'Brien's place, as it has no signpost and is almost obscured from view by vegetation. The track is bumpy and rutted and I wonder how they drive along it in the rain, when the ground will be a sea of mud.

Aidan O'Brien and his wife Siobhan arrived here from Ireland four years ago with their four children. None of their children attended school, although the two youngest were of school age, being thirteen and fifteen respectively. At that time the older two children were sixteen and eighteen years old. Siobhan managed to convince the education department that she had home-schooled her children in Ireland and she was capable of doing the same thing here. No one really knew how to respond to her, so instead, she was left to get on with it and the children were kept at home. The truth is, the children didn't want to go to school in a country that was foreign to them and where they couldn't speak the language.

The O'Brien family lead a very private lifestyle and they keep themselves to themselves. It's hard to see any evidence of how they manage or what they live on, but people in this part of the world are used to eking out a living somehow, and they're no different from anyone else. The children are always very friendly and respectful when they do come into town, and as far as they're concerned, their father's word is law.

Most people, including myself, think the biggest part of their income comes from growing cannabis. I'm sure Aidan was one of the major suppliers of Stephen Gold's drug trafficking business and I think the killing of their animals has something to do with their involvement. No one would know this farm was here without prior knowledge of its location, and someone would have had to drive up this bumpy track to get anywhere near the livestock.

Everything seems quiet as I pull up at the house, but as I step out of the car two large, collie-like mongrels come running towards me, barking. The door of the house flies open and a young man holding a shotgun comes running out.

"Who's there? What do you want? I have a gun," he yells. It's Collum, Aidan's oldest son.

"It's all right, Collum," I shout and hold my hands in front of me. "It's Danielle, the police officer. Don't you remember me? Look at me, I'm in uniform."

Slowly he lowers the gun. "I'm sorry, Danielle," he says. "We've had some trouble here. I didn't mean to frighten you."

He calls to the dogs and they now approach me with their tails wagging.

"Is your father at home?" I ask.

"He should be," Collum replies miserably. "He went away on business with Jean-Luc and he should have returned yesterday. My mother is frantic with worry. I suppose you heard about our animals?"

"That's why I'm here," I reply. "Where's your mother?"

"She's gone over to visit Jean-Luc's wife to find out if she's heard anything, but she should be home soon. Do you want to come inside the house and wait for her?"

I decline the offer, instead asking him to show me where the animals had been kept and he leads me around to the back of the house. Apart from one narrow field which is immediately adjacent to the house, it's impossible to see the rest of their land. Tall trees and thick vegetation obscure their other fields from view and Collum only shows me the area immediately behind the house.

I don't want to frighten the young man, but it's clear to me that these animals were slaughtered as some kind of warning to the family. There's no way the killer would have taken the chance of meeting Aidan when he was armed with a shotgun. They must have known he would be away from home at the time.

"None of the family heard anything, and the dogs didn't bark?" I ask.

"The dogs were inside the house with us because Dada was away. And the animals' shelters are all at the back of the field, which is a distance from the house, so we heard nothing. What kind of sick person would kill innocent creatures?"

I say nothing, but I know very well the type of person who would do this sort of thing and this boy's father is probably with him now.

"I cannot wait any longer for your mother," I say. "But please, get one of your parents to call me when your father arrives back from his business trip, so I know he's returned safely. I'll give you my card with the telephone number of my office, in case you need to get in touch with me."

He thanks me and takes the card. His expression is one of pure misery and I'm sorry for the boy. There's no point in me staying here any longer, as there's nothing else for me to see, so I get into my car and drive back to town. I hope someone from the family telephones soon, to tell me Aidan has returned, because I think there's a very real danger that he's gone the same way as his animals.

Chapter 9

When I return to my office it's nearly lunch time and I'm pleased to find that the young officers have completed all the work I left for them. They've also managed to handle several enquiries and one minor traffic incident. I'm still not sure what to do about the dead livestock, or the elusive Monsieur O'Brien, so I type a brief report on the incident for the file and head out for lunch.

It's such a glorious day, I decide to treat myself to a plate of mixed cold meats and a salad at the café, and when I arrive, I sit at an outside table in the sunshine. I'm amused by Madame Martine who is the proud owner of two black Scottie dogs. She calls her dogs 'the twins' because they were born at the same time and were the only two females in the litter.

As Madame Martine walks towards the café, her dogs, which are not on leads, walk side by side in front of her. Their steps are in time with each other as if they are joined by an invisible thread, and when they arrive at her chosen table, they each jump up onto a chair beside her. Madame Martine then produces matching bowls which she places on the table in front of her dogs. When her meal arrives, a portion of food for each dog also arrives and she scrapes it into their bowls. Then they eat their food, just like a family dining together. When the dogs have finished, Madame pours water into the empty bowls and they sit patiently while she drinks her coffee, until she is ready to leave.

People who are not of this town, and who don't know Madame Martine and the twins, are quite astounded to see them sitting at the table having their lunch. In fact, sometimes tourists get quite upset when the dogs are served at the table. But that is too bad, because to Madame Martine, these dogs represent the children she never had and one would never banish one's children from the dining table. There are many things in this town that are quirky and different from anywhere else, but that suits us very well and we wouldn't want to change.

As I sit in the sunshine and eat my food, I notice a black Mercedes driving slowly along the street in my direction and I realise that it's the same car I ticketed on Bastille Day. As it nears the café, it slows almost to a stop then the back passenger door is thrown open. A man is bundled out, he rolls onto the road then the car roars off at speed. He's very dishevelled, his suit is crumpled and dirty and it looks as if he's crawled through undergrowth in it. His face is grubby and bruised, but it only takes me a moment to recognise that it's Aidan O'Brien.

I leap up from my chair and run over to help him to his feet. He seems disorientated, so I hold his arm, lead him to my table, and give him water to drink. He gulps it down as if he's not had a drink in days.

"Aidan, are you hurt?" I ask. "What's happened to you?"

"I-I'm-I'm okay," he stutters a reply. "I just fell as I stepped out of the car. Everything's okay."

"You didn't just fall, Monsieur. The car didn't even stop properly. You could have been injured. Was that Edvard's car? Has he hurt you?"

"I'm fine, Officer, please don't make a fuss. I'm okay. I just need to call my wife to come and take me home. I just want to go home." He wipes a mixture of tears and perspiration from his face with his hands.

"I'm sorry to tell you, Aidan, but there's been an incident at your house," I say. "Someone has killed your livestock and your family have been very worried about you because they expected you home yesterday."

"Is my family all right? They're not hurt, are they?" There's a look of sheer terror in his eyes.

"Everyone is safe," I assure him. "But they're understandably upset about the animals."

"Thank God. Oh, thank God," he says with a sob in his voice.

"Now would you please tell me what's happened to you?" I ask.

"I'm sorry," he replies. "But I can't. I can't tell you anything."

He's obviously too frightened to talk about it, so I try asking a different question.

"Where's Jean-Luc? I thought you both went off to Spain in his van."

"Don't worry, Jean-Luc's fine, he should be home soon. They left him in Spain and just took me in their car. He's absolutely fine. I don't want to talk any more, I just want to go home. I'm going inside to phone my wife. Thanks for helping me," he says and rises to his feet.

He staggers and stumbles inside. I have no reason to detain him, so I let him go. I plan to question him and Jean-Luc about what's happened, but I don't hold out much hope of an answer. It was definitely Edvard's car Aidan was dumped out of and that worries me greatly. I have an ominous feeling of impending doom. It casts a shadow over this bright sunny day.

Chapter 10

Many people approach my table once Aidan disappears inside to use the phone. They all want answers to the same questions. They all want to know what happened to him and if the car from which Aidan was dumped belongs to Eddy the Red. Some people hold genuine fears, but most just want the gossip. I explain to them that I don't have the answers they seek but assure them that I will investigate. Then I make a hasty retreat to the safety of my office.

When I get in, I telephone Patricia at the funeral directors where she works because I want to hear a friendly voice. We've been attending an evening dance class at the community centre once a week and, when I speak to her, she asks if I mind her bringing her colleague from work to join us tonight. For a moment I'm guarded because I assume her colleague is female and I wonder if she might be arranging a date for herself. Neither of us has dated since we moved in together and I'm rather nervous about introducing a new person into our lives. However, when she tells me her colleague is named Claude I know this won't be an issue.

After I hang up, one of the junior officers hands me a piece of paper with a list of telephone calls I've missed. I see that the second number belongs to Siobhan O'Brien. The note beside it says that Jean-Luc has arrived home, but there's still no sign of Aidan. I don't feel it's necessary to call her back because by now she'll know he's returned.

Another call is to remind me of the date for the summer cycle race so I can arrange for extra police officers to be on duty. The third call concerns the date of the Charity Committee's meeting to make arrangements for the annual *vide grenier*. They're expecting the maximum amount of car-boot sellers to attend, so I'll have to put parking restrictions on the area they wish to use, to ensure there'll be room for all the vehicles taking part. The Committee has asked me to attend their meeting and I must try to accommodate them.

One of my colleagues has just placed a cup of coffee on the desk in front of me, and I have the phone in my hand to make a call, when I hear a commotion in the street outside. There seems to be a large, noisy crowd gathering and several drivers are pumping their car horns. When I step out of the office, I realise it's a wedding party.

The bride and her groom are being transported in a horse and carriage which is covered in bows made of ribbon and small bunches of flowers. I recognise the bride as she works at the Mayor's office. I know she's just twenty years of age and barely out of high school. Her groom's not much older. I wonder how they know, at that young age, that they'll want to be together for the rest of their lives.

I'm thirty and I've yet to go on a proper date. Perhaps I'm not cut out for married life. Perhaps I'm destined to remain single. Patricia and I are a bit like a married couple in a way. We're the best of friends and we support each other. There are never arguments in our home as we both like the same things. The only difference is that Patricia is a lesbian and I am not, so we'll never have a physical relationship. However, in all other ways, my life suits me very well and I'm sure it also suits my friend.

My attention is drawn back to the wedding procession. Many cars are following the bride's carriage and the door handles have been tied with ribbons which are fluttering in the gentle breeze. Car horns are still being honked and a horde of people are walking or running alongside the vehicles, cheering the bride and groom. Handfuls of coloured confetti are being thrown into the air, giving the whole procession a carnival atmosphere.

The bride looks radiant and her groom triumphant. Their respective parents are travelling in an open-topped car which is following the carriage. The bride's father keeps leaning out of the car to shake people's hands. The groom's father is playing tunes on a small accordion and the crowd are joining in with singing. It's a delightful spectacle and a day, I'm sure, the couple will remember all their lives.

After everyone passes by and the laughter and the singing disappear into the distance, all that is left is a fluttering of confetti, so I step back into my office and try to remember who I was about to telephone.

Chapter 11

I'm glad when my working day is over. When my colleagues leave to go home, I lock the office then go into the toilet to quickly change out of my uniform and into a pair of slacks and a t-shirt for my dance lesson. Patricia will meet me at the Community Centre where the class is to be held. It's a short drive over the bridge and when I arrive at the hall, Patricia is already there. She introduces me to her colleague who is a tall, slim man with straight, brown hair and serious eyes. Claude is rather nervous and he explains to me, that like Patricia and I, he is single and in his thirties. He tells me he finds it difficult to meet women in his line of work as, apart from Patricia, all of the people he works with are men. It would obviously be difficult for him to chat to someone at a funeral, when they are grieving and he is working.

I'm about to place my handbag on a chair beside Patricia's things when I notice a dog tethered to the armrest. It is the oddest looking dog I've ever seen. It's no particular breed, but looks as if it's been put together from all the rejected bits of other, better-looking dogs. It has ears like bat wings, a coat that sticks out in tufts in all directions and a skinny, long body supported by short bowed legs. Its tail reminds me of a toilet brush as it is slim and straight with a ball of tufts on its end.

"What a funny looking bag of bones," I say to Patricia. "Who does that sorry excuse for a dog belong to? Is it Claude's?"

"Um, not exactly," she replies.

"What do you mean by 'not exactly'?" I ask suspiciously.

She continues. "Claude and I were just stepping out of the shop when an old gentleman collapsed in the street. Claude immediately called for the *pompiers* and we tried to help the man. He was quite incoherent and kept talking about Napoleon. When the *pompiers* arrived the paramedic didn't think it appropriate to carry him into our shop. They thought the shock of finding himself being carried into a funeral parlour might just finish the old boy off. So instead, they tended to him in the street until an ambulance arrived to take him to the hospital in Ceret."

"That doesn't explain the dog," I say. "What's this dog doing here?"

"Well, he belongs to the old boy of course," she replies, as if I'm stupid not to realise this.

"So is Claude looking after it until the old man recovers?" I ask.

"Oh no," she replies "Claude wouldn't know what to do with a dog. He can barely look after himself. The dog is coming home with us. I'm not sure of his name, but the old man kept muttering something about Napoleon so I've been calling him that."

I stare at her in disbelief. She smiles back at me with a happy expression on her gentle face and I know, in that instant, I cannot refuse her. But I have this awful feeling in the pit of my stomach that Napoleon might be with us for rather a long time.

The dance teacher arrives and calls the class to order and for the first time since we started coming here there are enough male dance partners to go around. I find myself partnered with Claude for the evening and I thoroughly enjoy our conversation although my poor feet suffer greatly. At the break Claude and I sit together while Patricia takes Napoleon for a short walk and gives him a drink of water. Claude explains to me that he has worked for the funeral director since he left school and is now second in command of the business. He was awarded a junior partnership last year as Monsieur Porcel, the owner, has no family to take over the business when he retires.

"Arranging funerals is very lucrative," Claude says. "Because this town is a spa town, it attracts many elderly residents and visitors. An older population is a licence to print money in my business."

I think the conversation is rather strange in a gruesome sort of way, but I can't help liking Claude. He has a gentle manner that I find very appealing. During our conversation, we realise that next week we're both due to have the same day off, so he suggests meeting up for lunch and I agree. I find Claude interesting and I'd like to get to know him better as I don't have many friends. Patricia obviously likes him or she wouldn't have invited him to the dance class.

When the class resumes my feet take another battering from a very apologetic Claude. He might well become my friend, but alas, he'll never make a dancer. I'm relieved when the class is finally over and I can take my bruised toes home for a long soak in a basin of warm water. We say our goodbyes and Patricia and I head for home in my car, with Napoleon sitting comfortably on the back seat.

Chapter 12

It's been three days since the dance class and in that time, Napoleon or Ollee, as he is now known, has taken over our home and our lives. It turns out that the old man who collapsed in the street had never seen the dog before in his life. The dog had simply run to his aid, as had Patricia and Claude. Nobody has come forward to claim Ollee and he has no microchip or tattoo to identify his owner, but I'm not surprised. He's such an odd-looking dog that he wouldn't be one's first choice, or even one's sixth choice of a pet, but Patricia loves him. The dog follows her everywhere, and when she goes to work, she leaves him in the garden with food and water and the shelter of the lean-to at the back of the house. When she returns, he practically bowls her over with delight. I can honestly say that this little dog is the first and only male Patricia has ever fallen in love with and it seems he's here to stay.

It's a lovely day, so I decide to leave the office and take a walk along the main street. The town is full of tourists and there's a very pleasant holiday atmosphere. I see my friend Byron is sitting outside a little bar having a cup of coffee and I stop to talk to him. Brigitte, the owner of the bar, immediately comes over and places a cup of coffee on the table in front of me.

"On the house, Danielle," she says.

I thank her and take a seat beside Byron and we discuss his current business project. After a few minutes we see Edvard's Mercedes park almost immediately across the road from us and I notice Jean-Luc's van has pulled up behind it. Jean-Luc has a face like thunder as he jumps out of his van and runs towards Edvard's car. He wrenches open the passenger door and practically hauls Edvard out of his seat. I can't hear exactly what is being said, but I can tell that Jean-Luc is raging. Edvard's driver jumps out of the car and tries to calm down the situation. He's aware a crowd is gathering and I'm sure that's all that stands between Jean-Luc and a beating.

"I think I'd better intervene," I say to Byron.

"I'm coming with you," he replies heroically. "These are very dangerous men."

We stand up and start to cross the road. I can clearly hear some of the conversation between Edvard and Jean-Luc as we approach.

"Do you think I'm stupid?" Jean-Luc is shouting. "Do you think I don't know what you did to Aidan? You might scare him, but you don't scare me! I'll have no future business dealings with you. Do you understand?" He pauses for a moment and stares hard at Edvard, who doesn't reply. "I asked you a question, you useless pile of shit." Jean-Luc is too angry to be scared.

"Nobody calls me that," Eddy shouts back at him. "You're nothing but an illiterate peasant. Don't you dare speak to me in that way! You're not fit to lick my boots."

"This conversation is over," Jean-Luc replies and he turns to walk away.

Edvard reaches out to grasp him by the arm, in an attempt to stop him from leaving. "I'm not finished with you yet," he yells.

Without saying another word Jean-Luc swings round and head-butts Edvard in the face. Edvard drops to the ground like a stone. An audible 'oh' can be heard from the gathering crowd and people jump back out of the way. Edvard's driver tries to help him to his feet but the impact of the blow has rendered Edvard semi-conscious. I call out to Jean-Luc as he pushes past people but he climbs into his van and roars off, scattering on-lookers who have to jump out of his way.

I approach Edvard who is beginning to come round.

"Monsieur," I say. "I witnessed what has just taken place. Would you like to press charges for the assault?"

He leans heavily on his driver's arm and staggers to his feet. "N-no, no," he stammers. "No charges. I'll sort this out myself, just leave me alone."

"I'm warning you, Monsieur," I say. "You must do nothing to Jean-Luc that will constitute a crime. If you won't press charges, then consider this matter over. If anything happens to Jean-Luc, it will be you who I'll be seeking for an explanation."

"Pah!" he exclaims. "Get me into the car," he says to his driver. "And you can keep out of what doesn't concern you!" he spits at me.

I'm quite taken aback that he has addressed me in such a way, and in front of witnesses, but I decide to let the matter drop. I encourage the crowd to move on as Edvard's car pulls away from the kerb and disappears down the street.

"What an abominable man," Byron says. "Come back to the café with me, Danielle. Let me buy you a fresh cup of coffee. I thought you were very restrained under difficult circumstances and that probably stopped anyone else from being hurt. Admirable, very admirable."

"I should really go after Jean-Luc and charge him with causing a public disorder at the very least," I say.

"Quite frankly my dear," Byron replies. "I'd let the matter drop. Edvard lives in Spain, not here. With a bit of luck, he'll bugger off back there and we'll hear no more about it."

I'm inclined to agree with him because the truth is, I was scared out of my skin. I wouldn't like to tackle any of these dangerous men on my own, not unless my life depended on it.

Chapter 13

I'm having breakfast with Patricia and she's very envious that I've got the day off today. I've arranged for Claude to pick me up in his car, then we'll drive to the coast for our lunch as it's a beautiful day. He has agreed that Ollee can come with us and Patricia has a bag of things for me to take for him.

"Honestly, Patricia," I say. "That dog has more stuff than most children."

"But he needs all these things," she protests. "There are his bowls, one for water and one for his food, his food, of course, and a bottle of water in case you can't find any, his towel, in case he wants to go for a swim, and two of his toys. Oh, and his chew stick, in case he wants to gnaw on something while he's resting in the sunshine."

"This is meant to be a day out for me and Claude, not me and Claude and Ollee," I reply.

"You don't really mind, do you, Danielle? It would be such a long day for him, shut in the garden on his own, because I have to work until seven o'clock tonight."

I can see that she's beginning to get upset and I concede defeat. "It's all right, Patricia, don't upset yourself. Your baby will have a great day out and I'll even buy him an ice cream at the beach."

"Thanks, Danielle, I really appreciate it."

"Don't think I'm doing this for free," I say. "It'll cost you one of your apple pies. With Crème Anglaise," I stress.

She smiles and gives me a wave as she goes out of the door, then I hear her saying sweet things to Ollee as she passes him in the garden.

When Claude arrives to collect us, Ollee and I are waiting for him at the garden gate. Claude gets out of his car to greet me and he opens the back door for Ollee. The dog jumps in and takes up his usual position in the centre of the seat, so he can have a clear view through the window, by looking between the front seat passengers. He loves the car and gets very excited whenever he's invited to join me on a trip.

After a short discussion, Claude and I decide to head for Canet Plage because it not only has a beautiful beach, but also ample parking beside the long promenade that stretches the length of the sea front. Collioure would have been our first choice, but being the middle of the tourist season means parking would be impossible.

When we arrive at the beach, Claude manages to park right next to the promenade and we get out of the car. Before I can open the back door for Ollee, the excited dog has leapt between the front seats and he jumps out, pushing his way past me.

He stands staring at the sea for a moment before he leaps about, barking. It's clear from Ollee's reaction that he's never seen the sea before. He steps gingerly onto the sand and sniffs the air. Then he jumps about before beginning a mad run, round and round in circles, scattering the sand as he goes. Claude and I are laughing which gets him even more excited. He keeps looking at us as he hurtles around, to see if we're still watching him. He's like an excited child showing off to its parents. After a few moments he runs towards the sea but when a wave breaks on the shore and wets his paws, he jumps back and barks at it. Claude and I are helpless with laughter.

We spend over three hours on the sand then we put food and water in Ollee's bowls and place them on the ground. After he has eaten and drunk his fill, we dry his paws before we all climb back into the car. We've decided to make our way inland for our lunch as all the restaurants and cafes here are very busy with tourists.

Claude drives us to a restaurant in the village of St. Jean and we're fortunate to find they have a table free for us. Ollee manages to position himself comfortably under the table at our feet and before long, loud snoring can be heard from him. We enjoy a lovely four course lunch and we don't notice that we've been eating and talking for over two hours until Ollee wakes up and lets us know he wants to go outside.

I've had a lovely day and I can't wait to tell Patricia about it. When we arrive back at my house I turn to Claude to thank him. He grabs my shoulders and clumsily plants his lips on mine then he forces his tongue into my mouth. I can't move and I struggle to breathe. I feel stifled and I panic. I manage to turn my face away and shout at him to stop. He releases me and leans away from me.

"I'm sorry, Danielle," he says, "But I thought you liked me. It was just a kiss. What's wrong?"

"You can't just grab me like that, Claude," I reply. "I do like you. We're friends but I'm not ready for a relationship."

"It was one kiss, Danielle, that's hardly a relationship. I know Patricia's a lesbian but I didn't know you were. I'm sorry if I startled you, but you've been giving me mixed messages all day and I thought you wanted this."

"I'm not a lesbian," I reply. "I'm just not ready to be anything more than your friend."

"I've plenty of friends, Danielle and neither of us is getting any younger," he says nastily.

My eyes well with tears and I get out of the car and open the back door for Ollee. Then I gather up his things and I mutter a "thank you" to Claude and run into the house without looking back. I hear his car roar off as I close the door behind me. When I'm sure he's gone, I sink into a chair and burst into tears. Ollee comes over to lick me and he has such a look of concern on his face it makes me cry all the harder. When Patricia returns from work I tell her what's happened and I feel like such a fool. She's wonderful and kind and she tells me to forget all about it.

"I suppose he called you a lesbian," she speculates and my face burns. "Don't take it to heart, Danielle. Men say that when they can't understand why they've been rejected. They all think they're God's gift to women. Perhaps that's why Claude is still single. Perhaps he's just too pushy, you know; too 'in your face'."

I never thought about it like that because I immediately thought it was my fault for leading him on. I can always rely on Patricia to make me feel better about myself and I'm pleased to be back in the safety of my home and in the comfort of her friendship.

Chapter 14

Nearly a week passes after my disastrous misunderstanding with Claude. Patricia says he hasn't mentioned the kiss, but he has told her about the lovely day we had. She tells me he's talked about Ollee and the beach and our lunch at the restaurant at St. Jean. Patricia thinks he'll ignore the incident with the kiss completely and act as if it didn't happen and that suits me. I hope we can salvage something from our day out because until the unfortunate incident, I was having one of the best days of my life.

When we attend our dance class, Claude chats away to me as if everything is normal and I'm relieved. However, he doesn't dance with me, but instead chooses Rochelle who is a bit younger. She works in the library and she seems to be quite interested in Claude. When the class finishes at seven-thirty, she lets him drive her home.

The meeting of the Charity Committee is scheduled to begin immediately after the dance class, so I go and wash and change my clothes in the ladies' cloakroom then make my way to the small hall where it's to be held. Patricia is heading for the café. She'll have a glass or two of wine while she waits for me to pick her up and then we'll drive home in the car. We expect to arrive back at about eight thirty, and as it will still be light, we can have our evening meal in the garden.

The Committee are seated around the table when I arrive and I'm welcomed by them. They have the plan of the town spread out on the table, so we can discuss the arrangements with a visual aid. No one can calculate how many places can be sold for the car boot sale, because there's some argument over the length of the area on the river bank which has been chosen for the event. Eventually, with my help, we reach a figure of one hundred and twenty cars and this amount matches exactly with the figure that was decided on two weeks before. Then there's more arguing, while they decide how much to charge for each pitch and whether or not wine and beer should be sold at the refreshment stall. I'm tired and I'm bored and I wish they would stop arguing over petty things and let me go home for my dinner. It's very hot in the hall and I'm almost ready to nod off, when I'm jolted awake by a direct question from the Committee chairman, Monsieur Alonso.

"We would all like to know, Officer, how you propose to tackle the drug problem we're experiencing?" he says.

I wasn't aware of any drug problem and the question has come right out of the blue. "No complaint in relation to drugs has been reported," I answer cautiously.

"Is that so?" he continues. "Well, I'm raising the matter now. Tell Danielle about your boy, Denis," he says to the man sitting beside him.

Denis sits up in his chair and glances around nervously. There are nods of encouragement from several of the others at the table.

"My son attends rugby practice at the high school every week. He's a magnificent player and his mother and I expect that one day he'll represent our country." There are nods of agreement and mutterings from the others present. Denis continues, "Last week, when he arrived home from practice, I could smell cannabis smoke on his clothes, and when I asked him for an explanation, he practically bit my head off. He told me that many of the boys smoked cannabis and it was harmless. He didn't admit to smoking it himself, but I'm worried sick."

Madame Gault raises her hand slowly.

"You have something to say, Madame?" I ask.

"It's about my granddaughter," she begins. "She attends cheer leading practice at the school on the same night. My daughter said that she too, arrived home with her clothes smelling of the smoke."

Monsieur Alonso continues, "I've spoken to the man who lives in the mountains. Perhaps you know him, Danielle? We all know him as Jean-Luc, the pirate. He denies any knowledge of the problem and he became very angry when I asked him about it. We're sure he's involved in some way because Denis saw the incident between him and Eddy the Red. That gangster is definitely involved with drugs."

Denis nods in agreement before he continues. "I'm sure it has something to do with Jean-Luc and his business partner, the Irishman. We've always known that cannabis is grown in the mountains, but it was in very small amounts and it has never been offered to our young people before."

Madame Gault's hand is up again.

"Madame," I say.

"My daughter is frightened that other drugs might be brought into our town and we want to stop this problem before it escalates."

"Messieurs, Mesdames," I say. "I'm sorry, but my hands are tied. Until an actual crime is reported, there is nothing I can do except observe the situation. If one of you comes forward and reports a child for taking drugs, or if you observe the actual exchange of drugs for money, then I can bring charges against the perpetrator. But until that happens, I am in the same boat as the rest of you."

"If you won't help us, we'll have to tackle this problem ourselves," Monsieur Alonso says threateningly.

"Monsieur, it's not that I don't want to help you, but I cannot act on hearsay and I must warn you, if you break the law, I'll have to pursue you."

"Hmph," he replies. "You can lock up innocent people, but the guilty may go free. The law is an ass."

"Maybe so, Monsieur, but it's all we have. As I said, I'll keep a close eye on the situation and if you do have anything solid to report, I'll be delighted to act on it. Now if that is all, I'll say *au revoir*."

There are more mutterings from the table as I take my leave. I'm very worried about what they've told me because I've no doubt that everything they've said is true, but I'm not very sure how to handle the information.

Chapter 15

When I arrive at my office the next morning Aidan O'Brien is waiting at the door. "Well hello there, Officer Danielle," he says. "It's a grand day, is it not?"

"Bonjour, Aidan," I reply. "Yes it is a lovely day."

"Are you well, Danielle?" he continues. "I hope you're keeping fine."

"Yes, thank you," I reply. "And you?"

"Oh yes, yes I'm grand."

"Good," I say and we stand and stare at each other. He seems to have run out of things to say. I can't believe I'm making small talk with this man, I hardly know him and I don't like what I do know about him. I certainly don't approve of his lifestyle.

I unlock the door and enter the office, holding the door for Aidan. He stands and looks at me, but he doesn't enter. "Are you coming in?" I ask. "Was there something you wanted to see me about?"

He looks at the open door, as if trying to decide, then he speaks. "Right, yes. There is something I want to report."

He steps inside the office and I show him to a seat. The first thing I do is switch on the coffee maker, because I suspect I'm going to need a cup. Aidan is sitting in silence, watching me bustle about switching things on and opening things up. He declines a cup of coffee so when it's ready I just pour one for myself before sitting down at my desk and waiting for him to tell me why he's here.

"I suppose you want to know why I'm here?" he begins. "Well then, it's about my business partner, Jean-Luc. We were meant to meet up, but he didn't arrive and he hasn't been home. I think something might have happened to him. I'm worried."

"When were you meant to meet him?"

"Yesterday," he replies.

"Perhaps he got sidetracked. Perhaps he had one or two drinks," I say. "You can't deny he's gone 'missing' before when he's had a few drinks."

"This is different. We had a business meeting and his wife told me he left the house wearing his suit. You might as well know, Danielle. He had a run in with Edvard Albert a few days ago and Edvard threatened him. Jean-Luc told him he didn't want to work for him and Edvard wasn't happy about it."

I remember the incident I witnessed between Jean-Luc and Edvard and I too wonder if it has had something to do with his disappearance. I write down all the details that Aidan will give me, but he doesn't actually tell me very much.

"What kind of business are you and Jean-Luc involved in?" I ask.

"Oh, you know," he says, "this and that. We help each other with our farms. There's always something to do on a farm." His answer is very vague but it's all he offers.

"Are you involved with Edvard in business?" I ask him a direct question and he immediately glances away and can't meet my eyes.

"I don't want to discuss my business if you don't mind. I just want you to look for my friend."

"His wife hasn't reported him missing," I say changing the subject. "Perhaps she knows something that you do not about his disappearance."

"I've been to their house and I've asked her. The last time she saw him, was when he went out the door yesterday morning. She's not worried, because as you rightly pointed out, he does sometimes go off on a bender. But I know he wouldn't miss our meeting if he could possibly be there, and Edvard Albert is a very dangerous man to have as an enemy."

"Is Monsieur Albert in town at the moment, because if he's in Spain, I can't question him about Jean-Luc," I say. "Even if he is in town, he doesn't need to speak to me unless he chooses to, because I have no evidence of a crime being committed."

"So you're going to do nothing, then? I've reported Jean-Luc missing, but you're not going to do anything about it. I've wasted my time here." He stands up and he's fidgety and annoyed.

"Don't get upset, Monsieur," I say. "I plan to look for your friend and I'll file a missing person report which will be sent to all the police stations in the region. He's bound to turn up sooner or later."

The office door opens and one of my colleagues steps into the room.

"Sorry I'm late," he mutters and then he sits down at his desk.

I don't introduce him, instead I usher Aidan to the door.

"I'll telephone you if I discover anything about the whereabouts of Jean-Luc," I say. "In the meantime, if he gets in touch with you, do let me know."

As he's leaving he turns to me. "Please, please find him," he says. There's a note of desperation in his voice. "His disappearance scares me. This isn't a normal situation," he adds.

I watch him walk away from my office and I wish he'd explained why he's so frightened because, unless I know what's going on, it's very difficult for me to help him. On the other hand, I think, if I don't know anything I don't have to do anything, and given the people involved, I would prefer it that way.

Chapter 16

It is late morning and I've circulated the missing person report. There's no real evidence that anything is wrong but I've a nagging worry about Jean-Luc's disappearance that won't go away. The bad feeling I have concerning Eddy, and the escalating talk about drugs, is never far from my mind.

I'm delighted when the phone rings and it's Patricia. She has the afternoon off and as it's a beautiful day she suggests I go AWOL from the office and meet her for a picnic lunch by the river. My colleague can handle things here, and he can phone my mobile if I'm needed, so I agree and arrange the meeting time and place. When I finish the call, I let the young officer take his lunch break early and give him an extra half hour off. When he returns, I leave the office and make my way to meet my friend.

As I pass the *pétanque* courts at the riverside, a group of men are embroiled in a game. Monsieur Alonso from the Charity Committee is one of them. Before I can walk by, he calls out and asks if I have any information about the alleged cannabis dealers. When I advise him that I do not, he turns to the other men and they begin a heated conversation. I swiftly move on, because I don't want to get caught up in their chatter when they don't appear very happy with my answer.

I walk further along the track and soon I'm greeted by Ollee, who hurls himself at me, barking madly. Patricia is waving and laughing at the dog's antics, and I'm practically bowled over by his enthusiasm. It's a relief to be out of the office and I flop down on the bench beside her.

"Tough morning?" she asks.

"Very," I reply, and I tell her all about the missing man and the unfolding drug problem. It's a relief to get it off my chest. As usual, Patricia manages to put things into perspective and I'm able to relax and enjoy the superb picnic she's brought.

As we sit in the sunshine I observe two very large, well-built men heading in our direction. One of them is carrying a bag similar in shape to a tennis racquet and the other is carrying a rucksack. They nod to us as they walk past and we watch them as they head for the long grass at the river's edge.

"That doesn't look like fishing equipment," Patricia says. "I wonder what they're up to?"

We stare at them suspiciously until one of them opens the rucksack and produces glass jars, which he places on a large boulder. Then we laugh heartily when the other man produces butterfly nets from his bag and they both prance about, swishing the nets back and forth. It seems incongruous that two such huge men are butterfly collectors. Still, it takes all sorts, I think. I can't take my eyes off them because they look so comical. After a while I rise, walk over to them and strike up a conversation only to discover that they're collecting specimens for the university. Just as I return to my seat, I'm distracted by shouts for help, coming from further along the riverbank.

"Did you hear that?" I ask Patricia and she nods.

"I think someone's in trouble," she says.

I tell her to stay with Ollee and the picnic and I head in the direction of the cries. She wants to come with me but I don't want the dog getting in the way if there is a problem, so I tell her to stay put and not to worry.

"I'll be back in a few minutes," I say.

It's not long before I come across the source of the cries. A large group of walkers with walking poles has strayed into a marshy part of the riverbank and two of them have become stuck. Several of the group have slipped in the mud as they've tried to rescue their friends. They're equipped with lots of fancy gear for walking, right down to their designer backpacks and glare-resistant sunglasses, not to mention state of the art walking poles, but they're still in a mess. What a pathetic but hilarious sight, I think.

I don't want to get stuck in the mud myself so I call to them and let them know I'm phoning the *pompiers*. I can hardly contain my laughter when I make the call and the woman who answers the phone is giggling shamelessly. When I end the call, it takes only a moment or two before the siren sounds to summon the emergency services.

A number of people have come to see what's going on and, before I can stop them, two more have become stuck. After a few minutes I'm joined by Patricia whose curiosity has gotten the better of her. We watch helpless with laughter as the *pompiers* arrive and add to the chaos of the scene.

"I do hope you're enjoying yourself," a voice from behind me says. I turn to see a tall, muscular man wearing a *pompier's* uniform. It takes me only a moment to recognise Jean. He's a leading paramedic who helped me to solve a case at the start of the year. His assistance directly enabled me to get my promotion and for that I'll be eternally grateful to him.

"We meet once again," he says. "You haven't got any bodies for me this time though, Danielle. Just idiots," he adds, chuckling.

We exchange pleasantries and I introduce him to Patricia and Ollee. Then we all continue to watch the comical scene as walkers, paramedics and helpful busy-bodies slip and slide in the mud and the burly, butterfly collectors prance and dance around them, oblivious to everything but their prey.

Eventually the circus is over and so is my working day. I phone my colleague and when he has nothing new to report, I ask him to lock up the office and I head for home. The day has ended on a much brighter note than it began and I wonder what tomorrow will bring.

Chapter 17

A couple of days after my meeting with Aidan O'Brien, a report comes in that a body has been discovered at the foot of a mountain and I fear the worst. When I arrive at the scene the *pompiers* are already there.

"I shouldn't have made the 'no bodies for me this time' joke," Jean says with a wry smile.

"You know the old adage 'be careful what you wish for'," I reply, as my friend and I shake hands. "After not meeting for several months here we are together twice in one week," I add.

"The body is in a terrible mess," he continues. "You might want to stay back from this one. The man who discovered it has been sick and he's a hunter and used to seeing death."

"Is there anything to identify the corpse?" I ask.

"There's a card in his wallet with the name 'Sabatier' on it. Do you know him, Danielle?"

I feel a sinking in my heart because I know I must now get involved in a situation that scares me. "Yes," I reply. "His name is Jean-Luc Sabatier and he lives on a farm on the other side of the mountain. He was reported missing a couple of days ago."

"He's wearing a suit," Jean says. "I thought it strange for someone to be in this location in a suit. His shoes are missing, but I assume they've been knocked off his feet in the fall. As we had to wait here until you arrived, I sent a couple of my men to look for them. Once we discover where they've ended up, we might be in a better position to determine where he began his descent."

"You said that the body is in a terrible state. Why is that?" I ask.

"Firstly it is smashed from the fall, but more significantly, it has been eaten by wildlife."

The very thought makes me feel ill and although I know should be my duty to examine the corpse, I keep my distance, as Jean has advised. A man with a medical bag and a grim expression on his face comes puffing and panting towards us.

"Could he not have landed near a road?" he asks. "It was very inconsiderate of him to make me walk over this rough terrain."

"Bonjour, Doctor Poullet," I say and hold out my hand for him to shake.

"Bonjour, Madame, Monsieur," he replies, nodding. "We have to stop meeting this way."

This is as close to a joke as we are likely to get from the very serious Doctor Poullet. He too was present at the previous death I attended. On that occasion I made a fool of myself by asking naïve questions, but I won't make the same mistake twice.

The doctor approaches the body and sucks in his breath and I can see that even he is shocked by the state of it.

"You really should take some photographs of this," he says to me. "We'll need to document the position of the body before we move it."

"I'll take the photographs," Jean says gallantly. "There is no need for Danielle to get any closer."

"Can you tell us anything from your immediate examination?" I ask.

"I can tell you one thing," he replies. "This body was probably dead before it landed here. There is blood on the ground from the impact of his bones breaking through his skin, but if his heart had been pumping when he landed, there would have been much more."

A call comes from a *pompier*, who has located one of Jean-Luc's shoes and he's holding it aloft. I can see that he's climbed quite high up the slope and is standing under a rocky outcrop.

"He probably bounced off those rocks," Jean states. "I'll climb up there shortly and see if there's any sign of impact. Perhaps that's where he died."

"I doubt it," Doctor Poullet says as he examines Jean-Luc's head. "His skull has a large hole in it. The injury is inconsistent with the rest of the damage."

"How is that?" I ask.

"I think the hole has been caused by impact with a blunt instrument such as a hammer," he answers matter-of-factly.

"Could it have happened by his head coming into contact with a rock sticking out of the mountainside? Maybe like that overhanging piece above where the shoe was found?"

"Perhaps, it is possible but I doubt it," he replies.

I cover my mouth as I feel a wave of nausea rise in my throat. I can taste sick on my tongue.

"Are you okay?" Jean asks and he grabs my elbow to steady me.

"Yes, yes, thank you," I stammer. "It's just all so messy and brutal."

"Violent death is never clean and tidy. It would be much better if the corpse would simply lie down in a coffin for us," Doctor Poullet attempts another joke. "I have seen enough. This body can be released to the morgue. You will need to contact your superiors in Perpignan about this one, Madame, as it is likely to prove to be a murder."

I am not sure whether to be relieved or disappointed because dealing with violent deaths such as this that can get a police officer noticed. However, I'm afraid that becoming involved with this incident might be very dangerous and I don't wish to end up the same way as Jean-Luc.

"Don't take any chances with this one, Danielle," Jean says. "Let someone else be the fall guy if you'll excuse the pun. I have a bad feeling about this and my instincts are usually right. My Mama says I'm psychic and I always listen to my Mama. She's a wise woman."

"Thanks for the advice. I'll send an email to Perpignan," I agree. "But the truth is, until the death is proved to be murder, I'm in charge. Please let me have your report as soon as you can. I assure you, I'll be careful, as I too have a bad feeling."

I say my goodbyes to Jean and Doctor Poullet and I leave the scene as there is nothing more for me to do. I now have the grim task of informing Jean-Luc's widow of his death. She's a young woman with five children under the age of ten and a farm to run. I cannot imagine how she'll cope.

I decide to rope in Aidan O'Brien to assist me, as he knows the family. I'll have to inform him about his friend's death anyway, as he's the one who reported him missing. It will give me the opportunity to question him. If he has any sense he'll give me some answers and let me try to help him. I'm sure he's involved with Eddy the Red and I think he's in way over his head.

Chapter 18

I go back to my office and spend a few minutes writing an email which I send to Perpignan. I simply state that a body has been found, give the time and place of the discovery and the name of the hunter who found it. I don't mention the injury to the head or the possible identity of the body. Those details will keep for the time being. Then I sort out some work for my colleagues to be getting on with and I head for the O'Briens' place.

It is a long drive up the mountain and although I usually enjoy the beauty of the scenery, today I'm distracted. I have never before had to inform a woman that she has become a widow and I worry how she'll react. I ponder whether I should have a doctor with me, instead of Aidan O'Brien. What will I do if Monsieur O'Brien is not at home to accompany me and Madame Sabatier takes ill and I am alone with her and her five children? I'm out of my depth.

I manage to find a tiny strip of land at the edge of the road and I pull in and park. Then I phone Patricia. She is the voice of common sense and she'll know what I should do. I'm relieved when she answers the phone.

"When you inform the O'Briens' ask Aidan and Siobhan if one or both of them would like to come with you to speak to the widow. Although they know her well, they'll be in a state of shock and they might not want to come," she says. "If they won't accompany you and you're on your own, telephone Social Services. They'll arrange for the older children to be collected from school. They'll also call on Madame Sabatier and send for a doctor if one is needed. I suggest that someone, either you or one of the O'Briens', stay with her until someone else arrives to take over. She shouldn't be left alone today."

"Thanks Patricia," I reply, "As usual you've given me good advice. I may be late home for dinner because I don't know how long this will take."

"Don't worry, Danielle, dinner will keep and I'll put a bottle of wine in the fridge because I think you're going to need it. Good luck my friend. Sorry, but I've got to go. A client has just come in. *A bientôt.*"

I hear a click as she hangs up the phone and suddenly I'm on my own again. She has reassured me with good advice, but I'm still afraid of what I must do. The journey to the O'Brien's farm doesn't seem to take as long on this occasion. Perhaps that's because I'm less anxious to arrive this time. I turn into the entranceway and my car rocks and rolls as I drive up the impossibly bumpy track. Then I pull in and park close to the house. As I open the car door I can see Aidan standing at the doorway of the house and when I get out of the car, the dogs run up to me barking.

"Come away, you great beasts," he calls to them. "Come away will you!"

At the sound of his voice the dogs calm down and, after coming over to sniff me, they run off. Aidan steps forward. "Hello, Officer Danielle," he says, "It's a lovely day is it not? What brings you all the way out here?"

I am reluctant to speak, but I must. "Bonjour, Aidan," I begin. "I am sorry, but I seem to have found your friend."

"You are sorry," he repeats, trying to digest what I've said. His eyes widen and his body bends and he places his meaty hands on his equally meaty knees and hangs his head. "Oh my God, oh, my good God," he says "He's been hurt hasn't he? Someone has hurt him."

Siobhan steps out of the house. "Aidan, what's happened?" she asks.

"I'm afraid we've found a body," I say. "There was a card in the wallet that had the name 'Sabatier' on it. There's still to be a formal identification, of course."

Siobhan's hands fly up to her mouth. She holds her face and her eyes are wide with shock. "Oh, sweet Jesus," she says.

"But you saw the body, didn't you?" Aidan asks.

"I'm sorry, Aidan, but the body was unrecognisable. We'll have to wait for dental records to be sure that it's Jean-Luc."

"Oh God, Aidan, first it was the animals, now this!" Siobhan says.

"Is there something you want to tell me, Madame?" I ask. "Is someone threatening you? If they are, then surely it is now time to tell me and let me help you."

"Say nothing," Aidan practically spits at Siobhan. "We have nothing to report, Danielle." He works hard to regain his composure. "Have you told Jean-Luc's wife, Yvonne, yet?" he asks. "Maybe I should come with you."

"I'll go with Danielle," Siobhan says. "You fetch Jean-Luc's children from the school, Aidan. I used to be a nurse," she explains. "I'll be able to help Yvonne and I can stay with her because my children are adults and they can manage without me."

"Thank you, Siobhan, I'm grateful for your help. This is a very nasty business."

"I'll just get my handbag and a few things in case I have to stay the night," she says, before she disappears into the house.

I have one last shot at getting information out of Aidan but he's having none of it. "We are fine, Danielle, everything is just fine," he says unconvincingly.

Siobhan comes out of the house carrying a holdall and a carrier bag. "I've packed some food for the children. Just in case…"

Her voice trails off. She turns to her husband and tenderly kisses him on the cheek. "Take care of yourself, darlin'. I have my mobile, telephone me if you need me. I'll see you later when you fetch the children home." With that they share a brief kiss and Siobhan climbs into my car.

Before I drive away, I call out of the window to Aidan. "You'll have to come to the office and make a statement about where and when you were to meet Jean-Luc and what the meeting was about. I also want to know if anyone else was meant to be there. I'll get in touch over the next couple of days."

Aiden and Siobhan exchange meaningful glances before I put the car into gear and drive off.

"What a terrible business this is," she says to me. "I wonder if it will ever be over."

Chapter 19

It's lucky that I didn't have to find Jean-Luc's place on my own, because it's so far off the beaten track. If Siobhan wasn't with me, I wouldn't know that the narrow path which winds its way up and around the mountain leads to anything other than goat shelters. It's with some surprise that I see a wide hanging valley suddenly open up in front of us. A flat green plain stretches out across the mountainside and the house stands to one side of it.

There are clothes lines attached to a hook on the side wall of the house and they run between two spindly trees; Yvonne is hanging washing on the line when we arrive. She is *tres petite*, rail-thin, and the shapeless shift dress she's wearing hangs loosely from her shoulders. Her hair is mousey-brown and it hangs limply, framing her tired face. Two very young children are playing with toys on the grass at her feet. I glance at Siobhan and notice that her lips are quivering and her eyes are full of tears. I feel sick to my stomach as I park the car. I don't have a husband or a partner, so I can only imagine the grief this news will cause.

Yvonne watches us as we walk towards her. "What are you doing here, Siobhan?" she asks and she glances at me nervously.

"It's Jean-Luc," Siobhan answers.

She doesn't have to say another word. Yvonne looks at me and I nod at her, then she looks back at Siobhan. The washing drops from her hands and I manage to step forward and catch her as she sways and then sinks to her knees. She is skin and bone and her arms are covered in bruises, many of them weeks old by the colour of them. Hers has not been a marriage made in heaven, I think to myself. Siobhan gathers up the two children and takes them into the house. They know her well and they are happy to discover what treats she has in her bag. Yvonne comes around from her faint and she focuses on my face.

"He's gone, hasn't he?" she asks. "Jean-Luc is dead."

"Yes," I reply. "I'm so sorry."

"Whatever will I do?" she asks. She isn't actually speaking to me, she seems to be thinking aloud. "I have five children to support and I can't run this place. Who will take care of us? There's only enough food until the end of the week, then Jean-Luc will have to get the shopping. I don't have any money. He never gives me any money."

"Do you have any family I can call for you?" I ask gently.

"I have no one, only Jean-Luc. He wouldn't let me contact my family because they disapproved of him. I haven't seen them, or even spoken to them, for nine years."

"But they are still around and, I'm sure that under the circumstances, they'll help you," I reply.

"They don't know me," she answers. "They don't know about the children. I can't go home looking like this," she says, staring down at her bruised arms. "If they see me looking like this, they'll think they were right about Jean-Luc. He loved me so much, you know. It was always my fault when he beat me, because I pushed him too far. I always asked for things we couldn't afford and that made him feel inadequate and he got angry. It was always my fault." Her voice is barely a whisper.

"Aidan is going to get your children from school and bring them home and Siobhan is going to stay with you," I say. "I'll contact Social Services to see about getting you some financial assistance. You won't have to cope on your own," I try to reassure her.

"When can I see Jean-Luc?" she asks.

I don't want to be the one to tell her about the state of his body, so I refer her to Doctor Poullet. I manage to help her to her feet and I grip her elbow as we walk to the house. When we enter, I see that the place is spotlessly clean and very, very tidy. It's obvious to me, Jean-Luc ruled Yvonne with an iron fist. It must have been awful for her to live this way, yet she believes he loved her. She's borne him five children in nine years and she's worked like a slave in this isolated house. Dying was probably the kindest thing he's ever done for her.

"I'll have to return and take a statement from you, Yvonne, but for now I'll leave you in the capable hands of Siobhan."

I smile at Siobhan when I say this and she nods. I assure Yvonne, once again, that I'll contact Social Services about financial aid and I ask her to think about letting me contact her family. She's clutching a mug of coffee that Siobhan has made. Her hands are shaking so badly that the liquid is sloshing about and she can hardly drink it.

"I'd like to talk to you, Danielle," Siobhan says. "But not when Aidan is around. I don't want him to know. Maybe when you come to speak to Yvonne, you can speak to me as well?"

"Is there anything I can do for you just now?" I ask her. I'm hoping that in the clear light of day she doesn't change her mind.

"No, you're all right," she replies. "It'll keep."

I'd love to look around the farm, but as I say my goodbyes and make to leave, Aidan arrives with the children. We exchange a few pleasantries and then I get into my car and drive back to town. I'm happy to be leaving this sad place and my spirits rise with every metre I drive closer to home.

Chapter 20

I'm woken at six in the morning by the sound of the siren. The siren is a wartime relic that's still used today, as it's the easiest way of summoning the emergency services. I leap out of bed and reach for my mobile phone as it starts to ring. When I answer it, I'm informed that there's a major fire at the farm belonging to the Sabatiers. I dress quickly, scrape a comb through my hair, shout goodbye to Patricia and make for my car. I'm still sleepy as I drive through the narrow, empty streets of the town, then up into the mountains.

I can see the smoke from quite a distance away and I can taste it in the air. As I get closer to the fire, I detect the distinct aroma of burning cannabis. The cloying, sweet smell is not unpleasant and I can understand why people might smoke it. As I drive up the track to the house, I feel quite relaxed, and I don't know if it's because I'm still tired, or if I'm mellow from inhaling the cannabis smoke. I don't really know much about the drug. I've never had any experience of it, other than a brief mention at the police college, and it's been easy to ignore the dabblings of a handful of local people, especially as no youngsters have been involved.

A dark cloud of smoke hangs above the Sabatiers' home and the sky has an orange glow. When I draw up to the house the *pompiers* are already there and I can see Jean is busy shouting orders to his team. Siobhan and the Sabatier children are standing on the grass in front of the house. The children are wrapped in blankets and the youngest child is crying softly. A chair has been brought outside for Yvonne and she's sitting on it and muttering to herself. I can see now it's not the house that's burning, the fire is to the rear of it, behind a screen of trees. Jean approaches me when he sees me getting out of my car. "Hello, Danielle, we meet again," he says.

"Hello, Jean. Is something burning?" I ask, hiding my sarcasm.

"Cannabis, can't you smell it? There's a field of it behind the trees. Or at least there was before this fire. She started the fire," he says, pointing to Yvonne. "She's quite incoherent. I've called for a doctor. You'd be better off talking to the other one because she knows what happened." He looks towards Siobhan. "Fortunately, there's a water supply on the land or we'd have been screwed. The crop is about eight feet high and it's so dry at the moment that this house and a large chunk of the mountain could have gone up with it. Fortunately, the way the field's been laid out has created a natural fire break around it. We've been very lucky this time."

I take my leave from Jean and walk towards Siobhan and the children. I guess someone will have to talk to me now that I know about the cannabis.

"She's off her head that one," Siobhan says, by way of a greeting. "We might have burned in our beds. These babbies could all have been burned alive and me with them."

Her eyes are smarting from the smoke, as are mine, and I don't know if hers are watering, or if she's crying, but in any case, she's very upset.

"Can you tell me what's happened here, Siobhan?" I ask.

"I heard a thumping sound in the night and I thought I could hear an engine running, but it was outside, and I was in someone else's house, so I ignored it. Then I heard a whooshing sound and a loud bang. I knew that wasn't right, so I got out of bed.

When I looked out of the window I could see fire beyond the trees. I ran outside and I saw Yvonne. She was black with soot and she told me that she lit the fire. She kept repeating, 'They killed him. They killed him for that shit. Let them have it now'. That's what she said, 'Let them have it now'."

"Do you know how she started the fire?" I ask.

"Yes, I do," she replies, "Jean-Luc had about a dozen, fifty litre drums of petrol over by the field. They were lined up on wooden pallets. She took the screw caps off them then knocked them over with the jeep. The petrol spilled out and ran down the hill into the field. Then she lit it by throwing a bottle of petrol with a burning rag in it at the field. She told me exactly what she'd done. She was lucky not to go up herself."

"You told me that she kept saying, 'They killed him'. Do you know who she was talking about?"

"Edvard Albert. She was talking about Eddy the Red. He was threatening Jean-Luc, because Jean-Luc was refusing to sell him the cannabis he was growing. He didn't want to deal with Eddy because he's such a dangerous man. He's Albanian Mafia, you know. Eddy didn't just want Jean-Luc to sell him the cannabis, he wanted him to sell stronger drugs for him and Jean-Luc was having none of it. He wasn't scared of Eddy and he said that no one was going to make him sell drugs to children, especially not here where he lives."

"You'll have to come to my office and make a statement," I say. "I can't do a thing without a statement from you."

"Are you off your feckin' head? Do you think I want my family to end up like this one? I've told you what I know. I've told you too much already. Leave me alone now."

She turns away from me and I know the conversation is over. I'll get nothing else out of her because she's frightened, and rightfully so.

Siobhan has confirmed what I already suspected, but I'm not sure what to do with the information, or how much of it to use.

I'll have to report the fire and the field of cannabis to my superiors in Perpignan, but should I tell them more? I don't want to lose control of the case, but nor do I want to place myself in any danger. If Siobhan won't make a statement and if Yvonne does not, or cannot, confirm the link to Eddy, then I don't need to take the matter any further.

Now that Jean-Luc and the drugs are gone, there's nothing left for Eddy to want here. But if I'm to be brutally honest with myself, I know this business won't end because I'm sure Aidan is involved. I suspect Jean-Luc's death is some sort of warning to him and to the others Eddy intends to do business with. But why, I reason, should I do something today that I can put off until tomorrow? And why should I expose myself to risk, or get involved, before I absolutely have to?

Chapter 21

Over the last few days, everyone in town has been talking about Jean-Luc's death and the subsequent fire at his place. Everyone has a theory about who is involved and everyone knows someone, who knows someone, who is in some way connected to him. But by the time the report lands on my desk which suggests he was indeed murdered, his death is history and nobody knows a thing.

Siobhan O'Brien has, as expected, decided not to talk to me after all and her husband and children are never around when I call. Yvonne Sabatier and her children are being looked after by Social Services. She's had a complete breakdown, as after suffering years of abuse and virtual slavery at the hands of Jean-Luc, she can't function without him. Speaking to her is a complete waste of time.

I send an email to Detective Gerard, my superior in Perpignan, and offer to turn the case over to him because it involves murder and drugs. There's also the possibility of an international gang being involved, and if that's confirmed, I can't keep it to myself, nor do I want to. I'm surprised to receive no reply. I'm even more surprised when I arrive to open the office after lunch and find Detective Gerard on the doorstep waiting for me.

I invite him in and offer to make him coffee, but he declines. Instead, he suggests that we walk while we talk and I leave one of the junior officers in charge while Detective Gerard and I head off. We walk in virtual silence until we reach the opposite side of the river. He chooses an empty bench by the riverside where we're unlikely to be overheard and we sit down.

"Your email to me was straightforward and informative," he begins. "A man has been killed, probably murdered. The man grew cannabis on his farm and he possibly supplied another man who may or may not live in Spain. Am I correct so far?" he asks.

"Yes, that's right," I reply. I'd purposely kept my email short and to the point.

"Would you like to elaborate and tell me everything you suspect?" he asks.

I tell him about Edvard Albert and my feelings about his involvement. Then I tell him all that I know about the O'Briens, which is virtually nothing. I mention my meeting with the Charity Committee and their worries about cannabis being dealt locally. By the time I finish, I realise there's very little solid information to report.

"It was right and proper for you to offer this case to me," he says. "But I think that you've covered these matters very well yourself. I didn't want to say this to you in writing, which is why I am here in person, but it would be better if this case could just slip into obscurity. It is no loss to the world that a drug grower is dead. It is no loss that his farm has been burned. There's nothing left for his dealer to sell. Instead of spending a great deal of time and money on this case, when my budget is tight and there are bigger fish to fry, might I suggest that the file stays in the drawer. The truth is, I'm about to be audited and my name has just been put forward for promotion, so I don't want to spend any time outside Perpignan if I can help it."

"Are you asking me to do nothing?" I ask.

"No, of course not," he replies. "You must investigate what you can. Just don't make a big deal of it."

"What do I do if I uncover something important?" I ask.

"If the case moves on, you must of course keep me informed. And if you solve the murder, or you can prove that drug running is taking place, then I'll step in with all guns blazing. I can assure you of that. But for the moment, you are in charge of any investigations and I'll email you accordingly. In my email, I'll advise you that I'm sending you another officer to help lighten your work load, because you're handling this case instead of me taking over at this stage. Don't worry, Danielle, everything will be done by the book."

"I'd like you to officially appoint me as the investigating officer in charge of the murder," I reply. "I don't want to find myself out on a limb, but I do get your point about not looking too hard for answers. If we're lucky, everything will settle down as before."

"Of course, Danielle, thank you. We understand each other very well," he replies.

I'm excited to be in charge of the murder. Whether or not I solve the case is not as important as being given the responsibility of investigating it. It shows that my superior officer has confidence in my ability to handle things and that will look good on my record. The fact that I'm being allocated another officer to my team also strengthens my position and, best of all, I can do as little or as much as I like and still look good. When Detective Gerard leaves, I give myself the rest of the day off to celebrate.

Chapter 22

Over the next few days, I speak to anyone and everyone who's had dealings with Jean-Luc. My file on the case contains the report from the *pompiers*, the report from Doctor Poullet and the autopsy results. There are notes on an interview with Monsieur Perini, the hunter who found the body, a statement about the fire from Siobhan, which is very vague, and several recordings of missed appointments with Aidan, who does eventually make a statement, but actually says nothing.

A few local people insist on speaking to me, but they don't have information, they are merely speculating. I record it anyway. Some maintain Jean-Luc was murdered because of the cannabis field, some say it was because of the drums of petrol he had stored on his land, which turned out to be stolen. One of the ladies from the church committee tells me it was because he beat his wife. I explain to her that if that was true, several men who live in this town should watch their backs. She's not happy with me and storms out of my office.

By the time the weekend comes, I have a file full of effort and thoroughness, but not much else, to assign to the darkness of the drawer and probable obscurity. Detective Gerard would be proud of me, I think. I've carried out his instructions to the letter.

I don't really care why Jean-Luc was murdered, nor do I care that the case remains open. My only worry is that Edvard Albert will not give up on this town. I've seen nothing of him or his distinctive car, but much as I want to believe everything is now back to normal, I'm worried. People are concerned about local teenagers smoking cannabis and they're still asking me what I've discovered about it. I always remind them of the fire at Jean-Luc's place, and the burning of the cannabis field, which I unashamedly take the credit for. It stalls them, but they don't go away. However, by the time another week goes by, I'm able to walk through the town without being accosted, and I'm relieved.

Because I've now been sent another officer, I feel I must justify having him by putting him to good use. I've set him the task of religiously ticketing parked cars, where the owners have chosen to ignore the traffic meter and parked in restricted spaces. The drivers are all to be charged with causing an obstruction. The cost of parking is miniscule, but local people, who already pay their taxes here, hate having to buy a ticket. They argue that their taxes should be sufficient, and whilst I have some sympathy with them, they are still breaking the law.

My new employee attacks his task with gusto and after a few days, the whole town has something new to talk about. Brigitte, who owns one of the bars in town, complains bitterly. She tells me that I'm scaring away the customers who normally park in the street immediately in front of her bar. I point out that there are strict laws on drink driving and she quickly shuts up. Andre, who owns one of the *boulangeries* in the main street, asks why we don't make an exception of the cars with local number plates and simply ticket the tourists, who don't pay taxes here anyway. A nice suggestion, I agree, but I tell him that I cannot be seen to discriminate because to do so would break the law and I cannot break the law I'm paid to uphold.

After a week of vigorous ticketing, my new employee is being hissed at in the street and being made to feel very unwelcome. So I take him off ticketing duty and keep him in the office for a couple of days, sending instead one of the other young officers who has grown up in the town. I hope he is met with less bad feeling.

By the tenth day, everybody in town is moaning about the ticket machine. It seems to have taken on a personality of villainous proportions. By day eleven, a serious crime has been committed and I am shocked and dismayed. During the night, someone has vandalised the ticket machine. It is a piece of public property and I'm outraged that someone has abused it. White paint mixed with glue has been squirted into every opening, then the body of the machine has been painted from top to bottom with the same glutinous mixture. The paint pot has been left upturned on the top, like a trophy sitting on a shelf.

When I arrive at the scene with two of my colleagues, there are people milling about, smirking and giving each other thumbs up signs. Everyone is delighted by what has occurred, and of course, nobody knows anything about the perpetrator of the crime. Although one man does suggest it must have been a foreigner from Spain, because paint is very expensive here, but cheap there. A local, he reasons, would not have wasted good money, but instead would have used something else to vandalise the machine.

It takes all day for workmen to clean it up and even then, it still doesn't work. I place a sign that says '*en panne*' – broken – on the machine much to the amusement of all who see it, including my fellow officers. I'm annoyed because this crime makes a fool out of me, but there's nothing I can do. The only good thing to come out of this is that the people of the town have something new to focus on.

When I return home after work and tell Patricia about the incident, she is very sympathetic and serious, but after we share a bottle of wine with our meal, we both find we cannot stop laughing about it. I have visions of a clandestine band of elderly ladies and gentleman skulking about in the night, armed with their dangerous weapon – paint – and carrying out the daring attack on the machine. The more we talk about the incident, the more ridiculous and funny our conversation becomes and I'm glad I live in this house with Patricia. She always manages to cheer me up and I love her more than anyone else in the world.

Chapter 23

It's seven o'clock in the morning and I've been lying in bed, wide awake, for over an hour, listening to Patricia's singing drifting up from the kitchen below. I'll rise soon and go downstairs, but for the time being, I'm keeping out of the way as I don't want to get under her feet.

Yesterday I spent part of the day getting an area along the riverside marked out for the 'vide *grenier*'. My colleagues and I now have all the parking restrictions in place and we have marked out, with traffic cones, where the food and drinks will be served. I've also marked out the best pitch with cones and police line tape for Patricia.

She's managed to borrow a couple of small trestle tables from her work and some large, flat, plastic carrying trays from someone at our dance class. The trays are stackable and will be used to transport fruit pies. She's been baking as if her life depended on it and she now has over thirty pies to sell. If she sells them all, she'll be over ninety euros better off, even after paying the ten-euro donation for her pitch. She's hoping that once people taste one of her pies, they'll order them on a regular basis, just as they've done with her jams and bottled fruit. She is gradually establishing her own business and I'm proud of her.

Patricia had a poor start in life and was treated as an outcast from a very early age. As she became a teenager she was shunned because of her sexuality. I too was shunned and bullied at school because I was shy and I was dressed oddly by my mother. Like Patricia, I stood out from the crowd for all the wrong reasons. We became best friends and have remained best friends ever since. Now that we've bought this house together, our lives have improved beyond all recognition.

I hear the back door open and I assume she's now loading my car with her produce, so I quickly dress and head downstairs to help her. She's been practicing with the tables and the empty trays for days, so she knows exactly how to get everything into the car. My car is a Hyundai Tucson, and with the back seats down, it can hold an amazing amount of stuff.

Everything looks wonderful. Patricia's pies are packed in clear cellophane bags, so they are kept clean and the buyer can see what they're getting. I'm always worried about buying baked items at a market which have been exposed to the elements and had people coughing or sneezing on them. Patricia has solved this problem with her packaging. The plastic carrying trays have been scrubbed to within an inch of their lives and she has crisp, white, linen tablecloths to cover the tables.

When everything is loaded into the car and we've eaten breakfast, we get on our way. Ollee is sitting on Patricia's lap in the front and he's rather put out that his usual seat has disappeared. He's not a very small dog, so it takes a real effort on Patricia's part to control him. Every so often, he insists on leaning over and licking me on the ear, so it is lucky the road is empty.

The wonderful aroma of fruit, sugar and pastry is driving Ollee mad and I share his sentiments. However, we've both been warned repeatedly that we're not allowed to consume even a morsel of pie, as it would eat into Patricia's profit. The sale is due to end at one o'clock and as compensation for good behaviour, Patricia has left one apple pie at home to go with our lunch.

When we arrive, I remove the police line tape and traffic cones and pull my car into the space. Patricia is delighted with her pitch. Her tables will be set up at the start of the line and no one will be able to enter or leave without walking past her. I leave her to get organised and go over to the food stand where I see one of the members of the Charity Committee, as I want to check everything is in order.

Chapter 24

By nine o'clock, every pitch is taken and most people have set up their stalls. The Charity Committee has raised over twelve hundred euros, and on top of that, many of the local charities are represented with individual stalls. There are children's charities, cancer charities, and several different animal charities, not to mention charities to raise funds for everything from a school rugby team to a senior citizens' singles club. They are all here and they are all enthusiastic. From a rather grey beginning, it has turned into a glorious day. The food and drink stand is doing a roaring trade and so is Patricia. By ten-thirty, she has sold all but the last two pies, and by ten thirty-five, they've been bought by the singles club to eat with their morning coffee. Ninety euros to the good and with the money burning a hole in her pocket, Patricia packs away her tables and trays then she and Ollee join me for a walk around the other stalls.

One stall which appears at every market is the table manned by the Jehovah's Witnesses. I usually race past them to avoid taking their magazine, or becoming involved in a conversation, but today one of the members of our dance class is manning their stall.

He's a man in his seventies and his body reminds me of an aging matador. He has bleached, blonde hair cut in a very modern style. His hips are slim and he looks as if he's been poured into his well-cut trousers. His silk shirt is so fine, it's practically transparent and it's unbuttoned almost to his navel, revealing a smooth, waxed chest and a large gold medallion. He is like a caricature from the 1980's. Bertrand doesn't realise that a man of his age, and in particular a man with his style, isn't really the first choice of a girl searching for a boyfriend. He tries to stop every young woman who walks by under the guise of promoting his religion, but within a moment or two, the conversation invariably turns to him. He offers them lunch or dinner, or more disgustingly, breakfast after a night of passion; his words not mine. He invites them to the cinema or to the rugby or to the dance class. He is sex-mad, lonely and rather pathetic and, I think to myself, desperate and foolish if he thinks his charms can win over Patricia. The great gigolo does not seem to realise that being a lesbian means she's not attracted to any man, never mind him. Eventually, I manage to tear her away from Bertrand who, as a last resort, has given her one of his religious pamphlets.

As we continue our walk in the sunshine, we hear singing coming from a stall further along the row. The voices are in perfect harmony and I realise it's the church choir who are trying to raise funds for an orphanage in Africa. They're rather louder and more raucous than I would have expected, and as we approach, I see there are several empty wine bottles littering the ground beside them.

Patricia stops at the adjacent stall to negotiate a price for glass jars. The stall holder has about fifty which Patricia wants for her jam making. After much haggling, a price of five euros is agreed and we arrange to pick them up on the way back. The stall holder has a small poodle that Ollee takes a shine to and she seems to like him. But being a typical male, he helps himself to a drink of water from her bowl then abandons her for another more interesting woman as he runs after Patricia.

A bit further along the row is the inevitable stall selling live hens. We now have ten hens in our henhouse, most of them 'rescued' from the pot by Patricia. It's true that we do use all the eggs they produce, one way or another, but we don't have any need for more hens. However, I know it's not worth protesting and within a minute or two, Bertha, as she is now called, has been zipped into Patricia's shopping bag so that only her head is peeking out.

As we head back to collect the jam jars, a small group has gathered around the church choir's stall. They are laughing and joking and seem highly amused. When we approach, I can understand why. The choir master is leading his group in some of the bawdiest songs I've ever heard. They are all drunk apparently, and singing at the top of their voices.

I leave Patricia for a moment and run off to find one of the event organisers and I explain to him what's happened. He assures me none of the choir will be allowed to drive themselves home and that he, personally, will take responsibility for them. He's very embarrassed because his sister is a member of the choir and he tells me she'll be mortified tomorrow when she sobers up.

I'm about to go back to Patricia when I notice a group of young people with their bikes. They're gathered around a helmeted motor cyclist and there seems to be some kind of transaction taking place. I don't know why, but all my suspicions are suddenly raised. I don't like the look of it. There's something clandestine about the way they're conducting themselves. They're glancing about nervously and something is passing from hand to hand.

It's then that I notice a familiar car parked at the top of the hill. It's very distinctive and I recognise it as belonging to Edvard Albert. As I walk towards the group, the car horn is pumped and they all look around at me. Before I can reach them, they scatter and the motorcyclist roars off up the hill. The hairs at the back of my neck prickle and I have a sinking feeling in my stomach. I can't be a hundred percent sure, but I think I've just witnessed drugs being dealt to these teenagers. When I look back up the hill, the car has gone.

I can't get the vision of what I've witnessed out of my head. I put on a good show for Patricia, as she's having such a good day and I don't want to put a damper on it, but I'm worried sick. I don't know how to deal with this. I don't know what to do next, because I've never experienced this sort of crime. I want to figure out a way of protecting the young people, but I'm not sure how. One thing is clear however – I will have to do something, because much as I'd like to, I can't let this go.

Chapter 25

Over the next few days, I imagine that I see the biker everywhere and maybe I do. He always seems to be just out of reach, or just rounding a corner, but when I run to look, there's no sign of him. On one occasion, a similarly dressed biker came into the café and I was just about to grab him when he removed his helmet and I saw that it was a fellow police officer from Ceret. I'm becoming jumpy and paranoid.

People are beginning to question me again about the drug problem and I have to admit, if only to myself, that the problem is real. It's then that I come up with a brainwave, which will take the heat off me and possibly help the situation as well. I decide to start an anti-drug campaign, holding talks at the school and the clubs frequented by young people, in conjunction with a poster campaign. This way, the whole town can be involved and people will think they're doing something about the problem.

I send an email to Detective Gerard and request a small amount of funding to kick things off. I ask for two hundred euros, but I am granted only fifty with apologies and a reminder about his audit. The bare minimum I'll need is two hundred euros for the printing of posters and fliers. I write to various groups such as the Commune Committee and the Charity Committee, and within a few days, I've been promised six hundred euros.

Monsieur Autin, the local printer, offers to produce all the printing and posters at cost price. His son is in the cycling club and the school rugby team and he's desperate to be involved with the campaign. The Commune Committee offer to make all the arrangements for the public meetings and informative talks at the school and I let them get on with it. Everyone is rallying around and suddenly; I've become the town's hero. I'm stopped in the street by well-wishers. I no longer have to pay for my coffees or lunches in the restaurants and cafés and my picture is in the local paper, with information about the meetings. There's a strong feeling of camaraderie, and even though we're in the heart of the tourist season and our town is full of strangers, our community is solid and strong.

I'm surprised and delighted by the number of young people who attend the meetings at the school, considering it's the school holidays and I'm sure it's the last place they'd want to be. Many of the youngsters are wearing badges bearing the slogan 'Say No to Drugs' which were donated by a local businessman. A company in Perpignan has produced rugby shirts for our school team, sporting the same words. It's only been two weeks since the campaign began and already there's been an impact I couldn't have imagined.

I haven't seen the biker again, but to be fair, I haven't looked for him. Neither have I seen Eddy's car. As so much money and goods have been donated to the anti-drug campaign, I decide to use some of the money to buy myself two new outfits to wear when I am giving my talks. I feel as if I am entitled to this, and I also pay myself overtime out of the fund because after all, the meetings are work for me. During each meeting there is a break for coffee and I always purchase some of Patricia's homemade fruit pies for this event. All in all, I am doing rather well out of the campaign, both materially and emotionally.

It's mid-morning on yet another lovely sunny day and I'm standing in the street chatting to one of my colleagues, when I notice my mother making her way towards me. I haven't seen her for some weeks, but that's as much her fault as mine. She prefers not to see me, choosing instead to talk about me and criticise me to her cronies. Her constant disapproval of my job, the way in which I conduct myself and my life in general, is a heavy burden on me and it's easier not to have much contact with her. I do, of course, still see my father, but only when we bump into each other in the street, never at my home or his.

Perhaps she is at last, going to praise me for something. Perhaps I've finally done something she approves of. After all, the whole town is talking favourably about the campaign and I'm frequently front page news. I feel nervous and I experience a jag of fear and anticipation as she draws nearer.

She stops about two feet from me, "Danielle," she acknowledges.

No 'Dear Danielle,' or 'Çava va, Danielle', not even a 'Hello'. She simply says my name, and hearing her say it, brings a lump to my throat and I fear I may cry. All my life I've sought her approval and all my life it's been denied to me.

"How are you, Mother?" I manage to say. "You're looking well," I lie.

In truth, she has aged. I'm shocked by her old fashioned, shabby clothes and grey hair and the way her body stoops. She's not very old, but she looks ancient. It's as if all her bitter words and spiteful deeds are destroying her from the inside out.

"You ask me how I am," she replies, "as if you care. You don't care if I live or die. You've always been selfish and that has not changed."

My colleague shifts uncomfortably from one foot to the other before excusing himself and practically running away from us. He's embarrassed and I can understand why. I too am embarrassed, but I feel I must stay and hear what my mother has to say. I'm still hoping for some recognition of my work, but I've given up on hoping for praise.

"I want you to know that I've seen you in the newspaper," she continues. "Why must you always push yourself forward like that? It's embarrassing for me to have to explain to people why my daughter is constantly drawing attention to herself. It would be different if you weren't taking a job that should rightfully be a man's. It might even be different if you were married and not living with a lesbian. The way you live your life is a sin, but you are still my daughter. You are my cross to bear and I pray every day to God that he will have mercy upon you."

I stand in shocked disbelief, unable to utter a single word. I'm outraged by her verbal attack. Even after months of living in my own home and finding happiness there, a few sentences from my mother can reduce me to a miserable wreck.

How dare she criticise me? How dare she hurt me again? It's taken me years to realise her vile hatred is her problem and not mine. How dare she seek me out, only to break me down again? Without another word she turns and walks away and I'm left reeling. I am angry at myself, for once again feeling like a vulnerable child and leaving myself open to attack.

"Danielle, Danielle. Are you all right?"

Words cut through the haze.

"Are you okay, Danielle? You're a ghastly colour. Are you ill?"

I manage to focus and see Byron standing beside me. He takes my arm gently.

"I thought you might pass out there for a moment, but your colour's coming back now. Was that your mother you were talking to? I thought it looked like her."

I nod. "She's praying for me," I reply with a wry smile.

"Oh dear, well I'd better offer you something stronger than a coffee then. Ricard, at the café? Will you join me?"

I thank him, but refuse his kind offer. I've got an overwhelming urge to return home. I want to feel safe and my home has a healing effect on me. I want to absorb the warm atmosphere within its walls.

Chapter 26

The journey passes in a blur. Too late, I think of all the things I should have said to my mother. I still can't quite believe she's done this to me once again, and as I park the car and step into the garden, I'm close to tears. Ollee hurtles towards me with his favourite toy, a burst football, in his mouth. He bangs the ball into my knees in an effort to get me to play with him, but I'm really not in the mood for games. I half heartedly pull the ball from his jaws and throw it far down the garden and the little dog careers after it. Then I enter the front door and slump into my chair. I feel exhausted, even though I've done very little work. It'll be another five hours before Patricia gets home from her work. I could tidy up the house or do a bit of gardening, but I simply can't summon the strength, or the will, to begin. Instead, I find myself overcome by sleep and I succumb to it.

I'm woken with a start when Ollee's ball is dropped into my lap. I hadn't realised I'd left the front door open, but I must have done. The little dog is whining and pawing at me, trying to get me to play with him. I feel rather disorientated and it takes me a moment or two to realise where I am. When I look at the clock, I'm surprised to see that I've slept for three hours. I move from the chair and put on some coffee to help me to come to, as I always feel a bit woozy when I wake from an afternoon nap.

Then I step out into the garden to get some air and spend a few minutes playing with Ollee.

I try to put my mother's unkindness out of my mind, but it lurks there like a bad smell and I can't wait for Patricia to come home. She has the ability to put things into perspective and she always manages to cheer me up when I've had a bad day.

I happen to be looking out of the window when Patricia arrives home and I'm surprised to see she has someone with her. She didn't say anything when she left for work this morning about bringing anyone home for dinner, and I don't recognise the woman who's laughing and linking arms with my friend. They seem to be very chummy and I'm instantly on guard. I'm shy with strangers and I'm not sure what the relationship is between Patricia and this woman. From the way they're looking at each other, and the way they're interacting, I suspect their relationship might be more than platonic, but Patricia hasn't mentioned anything about a new friend. I feel rather put out that Patricia has brought her to our home without first asking me how I would feel about it, or indeed, even informing me in advance. Both women enter the house in a flurry of gestures and giggles and hugging and perfume.

"This is Claire," Patricia says in an offhand way, nodding towards her companion. "She's staying for dinner."

Claire is a woman of about forty years of age. She has a thin face with cat-like features and her body is petite and angular. She has a hard expression in her eyes which remains, even when she's smiling. I take an instant dislike to her.

Patricia has not said 'hello' to me or kissed my cheeks, which is our usual greeting when we see each other. Before I can say anything to her, Claire speaks.

"Ooh, I do like a woman in uniform," she says, then leers and winks at me.

Patricia touches her arm and they both laugh. I don't find the woman funny, quite the reverse in fact. She makes me feel uncomfortable in my own home and in my own skin.

Claire flops down in my chair without being invited to sit and Patricia busies herself in the kitchen. I still have had no explanation as to who Claire is, or what she's doing here, and I feel hurt and put out.

"You two have a chat while I make the dinner," Patricia calls.

It seems that I'm to entertain her guest and I'm not happy about it.

"Sorry, Patricia," I reply. "I'm just going to get changed then I'm out of here. I've an appointment in town and I'm eating there. I won't be home until at least eleven o'clock and then I'll be going straight to sleep, as I have a long day at work tomorrow. Perhaps we will 'chat' another time."

"You didn't mention anything about an appointment in town," she replies critically.

"You didn't mention anything about your friend coming for dinner. A slight breakdown in communication it seems."

There's an uncomfortable silence as I turn and head upstairs to my room. I know I'm acting childishly, but I'm annoyed and I don't want to be the extra person at the dinner table, or be made to feel like a guest in my own home. I quickly get washed and changed, gather up my bag and my phone and make for the door. As I leave I shout a vague 'goodbye' and quickly slam the door without waiting for a reply. I'm not quite sure where I'm going, or how I'll fill the next few hours and I really don't want to be alone.

I get in my car and drive a couple of hundred metres from the house and park. Tears are streaming down my face and I find myself sobbing. This has been a horrible day and now I'm stuck outside with nowhere to go, and the one person I need to talk to, is spending what should be my time with someone else. I feel so helpless and sorry for myself and I'm jealous of Claire and my heart aches. I love Patricia and I don't want to share her with anyone else.

I spend the next few hours alternating between driving around and hanging out in my car. I don't want to go into town, because I don't feel very sociable, and if someone talks kindly to me, there's a very real risk that I might make a fool of myself by blubbering.

At eleven-thirty, I drive towards home and when I arrive, the whole house is in darkness. I enter as quietly as I can – Ollee raises his head from his blanket, offers me a small 'woof' and a single wag of his tail before going back to dreamland. I'm ravenously hungry, so I prepare some bread and cheese. There's still some of the meal that Patricia made in the pot, but I don't want her to know I haven't eaten, so I leave it where it is. I don't know whether or not Claire is still here, but I expect that she is, and I imagine her in Patricia's room, sharing her bed. After wolfing down my sandwich, I drag myself up the stairs, exhausted and miserable, and cry myself to sleep.

Chapter 27

I sleep fitfully then wake late to find that Patricia has left for work without calling me. This is the first time since we moved in together that we haven't spoken in the morning and I'm bereft. I rush around like a mad thing, then drive too fast to work and arrive there just in time for the office to be open to the public. The two policemen who are working for me this month are at their desks and they've already begun to deal with the morning's workload. I assume they can tell that I'm out of sorts as they barely glance up, but instead, work on in silence. One of them makes me a cup of strong, black coffee, which he places on my desk. I nod my thanks, and manage to take just one sip from the cup, before Aidan and Siobhan walk through the open office door in a very agitated state.

"Hello, Danielle," Aidan says "Can I talk with you?"

"It's our Collum," Siobhan adds, before I can answer, "he's missing."

She swipes at her eyes with a hanky, but she can't stop the tears from spilling down her cheeks. Aidan stands stiffly like a tightly-coiled spring. His interlocked hands are pressed to his rotund belly and his teeth are gritted. The only parts of his body that move are his eyes, which blink nervously. I invite them to sit down, usher them into the chairs in front of my desk, and ask one of my colleagues to pour coffees. I know they must be desperate, because I'm the last person they would come to for help.

"Tell me what has happened," I say.

They look at each other before Aidan speaks. "As Siobhan says," he begins, "my boy is missing. He's been gone two days now. It's not like our Collum to be gone for two hours, never mind two days."

Siobhan swipes away more tears with her sodden handkerchief and her shoulders are heaving with her sobs. "He rarely leaves home," she adds. "He's the man of the house when his Dada's away." She stares at me pleadingly.

"Have you any idea where he might have gone, or who he might have gone with?" I ask. "Does he have a close friend or perhaps a girlfriend?"

They both drop their chins and stare at the ground.

"Is there something you're not telling me?" I press. "I can't help you, if I don't know all the facts."

Siobhan looks up, "Well, there is something," she begins.

Aiden grabs her arm and stares into her eyes, as if silently warning her not to say too much. She snatches her arm from him.

"I must tell her, Aidan. I must! Collum might be in terrible danger. Remember what happened to Jean-Luc."

He exhales with a sigh and nods his agreement, for Siobhan to begin. "I was driving home a few days ago, and when I got to the track that leads to our house, I saw Eddy's black Mercedes stopped at the side of the road. I was scared, because I thought he was waiting for Aidan. So, as I drove along the track, I kept glancing in the rear view mirror to see if he was following me. Imagine the shock I got, when I saw our Collum get out of his car."

She stops talking as she is once again overcome with emotion and racked with sobs.

"When Siobhan came home and told me what she'd seen, I was very angry and scared," Aidan adds. "I don't mind telling you, Danielle, I was really shit scared. I know what kind of a man Eddy is and I don't want him near me, never mind my son, especially after what happened to Jean-Luc."

"Aidan was going to go down the track and fetch Collum home," Siobhan continues, "but, by the time he went inside and fetched his shotgun, we could see our boy walking towards the house on his own. When he approached us we asked him what was going on between himself and Eddy and he just shrugged.

"I tell you, Danielle," Aidan cuts in, "I was blazing mad. I asked him why he would be talking to a no-good gangster like Eddy and he snapped at me, 'For the money Dada. Have you seen the roll of money he carries? There must be hundreds of euros there'."

"Does Collum have any money of his own?" I ask. "Does he have any earnings?"

"He works with his Daddy," Siobhan says "We give him pocket money. We give all the children pocket money."

"But Collum is no longer a child," I point out. "He's in his twenties. Maybe he has a girlfriend. Maybe he needs more than just pocket money. Do you think he's gone with Eddy to Spain? Is that a possibility?"

"Oh dear God, I hope not," Aidan blurts out. "What can we do, Danielle? How can we find him and fetch him home?"

I rest my chin on my hand and my elbow on the desk and think for a moment. "I'll report Collum as a missing person and I'll contact a friend who works for the Spanish police. But I must warn you, even if I do find him, I can't force him to come home. He's an adult now and, should he be arrested in Spain, I'll not be able to intervene."

"Maybe I'll drive into Spain and find that bloody Eddy myself," Aidan says. "I'll soon fetch my boy back if he's there."

"That's entirely up to you," I reply. "But might I suggest the softly, softly approach first. Your boy could simply be blowing off steam and he might welcome a local Spanish policeman advising him to return home to France. Perhaps he's bitten off more than he can chew, but can't see a way out."

Aidan holds his head in his hands then runs his thick fingers through his hair. "You're right, Danielle," he replies and Siobhan nods her head in agreement. "That makes perfect sense. How long will it take for you to speak to your colleague? When will he look for my boy? I can't help worrying that the longer he's away, the more likely he is to get into trouble."

"My colleague works the evening shift, so I'll call him later today. Anyway, he's more likely to come into contact with Collum in the evening, so if you drop in a photograph of him, I'll scan it and email it to Spain. That way, when my friend starts his shift, he can look out for your boy."

Both Aidan and Siobhan exhale their bated breath.

"Thank you, Danielle. Thank you so much," Siobhan says.

"Yes, yes, indeed, thank you very much," Aidan adds and he grabs my hand and shakes it vigorously.

I ask one of my officers to write down Collum's personal details. Then I say my goodbyes to Aidan and Siobhan, gather up my bag and leave the building. I need to clear my head and I don't want to be trapped at my desk while Aidan and Siobhan are still in the office. I'm worried about Collum, because he's a very naïve and impressionable young man having spent his adult life stuck on a remote farm. I like the boy. He's polite, soft spoken and well-mannered and I don't want him to come to any harm. I hope that my friend in Spain can find him and scare him into coming home, before something nasty or criminal occurs. I have an ominous feeling of impending doom. The snakes are beginning to slither out of the box and I don't have enough hands to push them all back in.

Chapter 28

I'm so troubled by the rift between Patricia and me that I break all our rules and head for her place of work. We've agreed always to telephone, and not just turn up, when either of us is working but I'm frightened she won't take my call. I needn't have worried, however, because when she sees me she rushes over and hugs me.

"I'm so sorry, Danielle," she says, "I've been an inconsiderate idiot. Will you forgive me?"

I'm so relieved I want to cry. "I just didn't know what was going on," I reply. "I wasn't expecting anybody to come home with you and I'd never met Claire before. But of course you can bring your friends to the house. It's your home, after all."

"I should've said something first, but it all happened so quickly," she continues.

I don't ask whether or not Claire spent the night, there's time enough for that later, I think. "I was just being selfish," I say. "I'd had a really bad day and I wanted to talk to you because you always manage to make me feel better. I was jealous that someone else was taking up your time. I'm sorry, Patricia."

"Don't be," she replies, "I should've checked with you before bringing someone into our home. What did you want to talk to me about? Is it too late now?"

I'm about to speak when a very distressed elderly lady comes through the door.

"Sorry, but it'll have to keep until later," Patricia says. "We'll talk at home. Duty calls."

She hugs me and kisses me on the cheek, then propels me towards the door. "Love you, see you later," she says.

I find myself out of the funeral office and in the street and I feel as if a load has been lifted from my shoulders. I'm grinning like an idiot with relief. I feel so elated, that I spend the rest of the day being nice to people. I give directions to tourists, I pat stray dogs and I don't write a single parking ticket. I treat my colleagues to pastries with their afternoon coffee and although they eye them and me with suspicion, they devour them with relish.

At five o'clock I telephone my friend Paco, who works as a policeman in Spain, and tell him about Collum and Eddy the Red and the trouble we're experiencing here with drugs.

"We have many, many young people involved with drugs," he says. "It's a real problem in cities. Lots of young people flock to Barcelona, so it's a common occurrence here."

"Do you think you might come across Collum before he lands in trouble?" I ask.

"Maybe," he replies. "If he's as naïve as you say, we'll come into contact with him eventually, but whether or not we can send him home before he gets into trouble, is anyone's guess."

"Have you come across Edvard Albert?" I ask.

"Oh yes, we know him, but he's always managed to avoid charges. He's one slippery fish. If he has your young man in his power, he's unlikely to let him go. Many of his drug pushers are only selling drugs to finance a habit he's inflicted on them. I won't lie to you, Danielle, your young man is in real danger of disappearing into another world, a world where power is everything and life is cheap."

"Please do your best to find him for me, Paco," I plead. "I'm emailing you a photograph. Will you circulate it around to your colleagues?"

"Of course," he replies. "I'll do my best for you, but don't hold your breath. I can't make any promises."

I thank him for his help but I'm worried that Collum is lost to us already and I don't know what else to do.

When I arrive home after work, Patricia has dinner ready and the pungent aroma of her tagine makes me salivate. We sit down to dine and I open a bottle of heavy red wine which we gulp rather than savour. After a few minutes Patricia begins to speak.

"I must explain about Claire," she says. "We met just two weeks ago when she came into the office to sell us funerary ware. She's a rep and she's based in Perpignan. We had an instant, mutual, physical attraction. It's been so long since I had a relationship, a one-night stand seemed like a very attractive proposition."

She pauses and pours herself some more wine. She's obviously nervous telling me this and she's studying my face for a reaction.

"A one-night stand – so you don't intend to see her again?"

"We have nothing in common," she continues. "It was simply for sex, there won't be any relationship. It's over, a one-off liaison."

I feel uncomfortable speaking about this. "You don't have to explain yourself to me," I say.

"Yes, I do," she replies. "When I thought about it, I realised how appalling my behaviour had been. I had no right to introduce a stranger to our household in that way. If you'd brought some strange man home without consulting me, I'd have been outraged. I was driven by lust and I'm so ashamed of the inconsiderate way I've treated you. I promise you, it will never happen again."

"But you must be able to have dates," I protest. "What happens if you meet the love of your life?"

"Don't you understand, Danielle? You are the love of my life. If you were a lesbian, my life would be complete. You fulfil all my needs. I love you. I think that I've always loved you."

I'm stunned and delighted by what she's said. "I love you too," I admit. "I'm at my happiest when I'm in your company, but where do we go from here?"

"Well," she ponders, "We can agree that holding each other in a comforting way is okay, we do that already. But no kissing with tongues," she jokes. "There's no point torturing ourselves. A physical relationship is never going to happen and I accept that. If either of us wants a sexual encounter, it should be arranged out of our home. That'll avoid any further embarrassment. What do you think?"

"That suits me perfectly," I answer. "On cold winter nights, when we go to bed early to read, we can snuggle up together for company and comfort, just as we've always done. There'll be no awkwardness between us."

"Perfect," she replies. "I'm glad we've sorted ourselves out."

We eat our meal, and talk, and make plans, and drink more wine than we should. When we are quite merry, we go upstairs and climb into my bed, where we talk some more. Patricia eventually falls asleep and I don't wake her. I've gone from deep despair to elation. I'm so happy I could burst. My life is perfect in every way and nothing my mother or her cronies might say, can ever hurt me again.

Chapter 29

It's been over a week since Collum O'Brien went missing and Aidan has been to Barcelona several times to search for his son. Siobhan has become like a ghost of her former self. Her once rosy cheeks have grown hollow and grey and she seems to have shrunk with grief and worry. My friend Paco has not seen hide nor hair of the young man and neither have any of his colleagues, so I'm very surprised when I arrive at the office and find that I've had a telephone call from Byron about him. When I return his call, he tells me Collum has rented a ground floor studio apartment from him in the centre of town, and he's paid three months rent in advance, in cash. I immediately telephone the O'Briens.

After thanking me profusely, Aidan says, "You'd better be ready to arrest him, Danielle, because if he has that kind of money, he's been up to no good. My boy has never had anything more than pocket money and three months' rent is several hundred euros. Where would he get that kind of cash?"

I explain to Aidan that I can't just go around arresting people without any evidence of wrongdoing and I suggest he lets the dust settle before he confronts his son. At least he now knows his boy is safe, and has returned to town.

When I hang up, I leave the office and make my way into the town centre. Today's the day of the under eighteen's cycle race and my officers have closed off several streets to traffic. This is a well attended event and there's fierce competition between the entrants, who incidentally, are all young men. Some of the past winners have gone on to compete in the Tour de France.

The town is alive with people even though it's still early in the day. The cafes and bars are already doing good business and there are many groups of young people standing in the street, securing the best spot to observe the race and cheer on their friends. It's a proud day for the athletes and indeed, for the whole town. It's a celebration of our way of life and of our strong, healthy, young people.

As I wander around, I'm surprised to see Collum O'Brien standing and talking to one of the groups of youngsters. He looks very different from the last time I saw him. He's dressed in banana yellow cut-off trousers and a t-shirt of the same colour, even the canvas bag that hangs from his shoulder is yellow. He seems to be passing something to one of the youngsters, but I can't make out what it is. He's alerted to my approach by one of the girls in the group and turns tail and runs before I can reach him. As I near them, the whole group disperse in different directions and I'm left standing in an empty space.

It occurs to me that I might have just witnessed a drug deal and I'm horrified. He's obviously wearing bright yellow so he can be easily identified by his potential customers. What the hell do I do now? I'll have to think about this, because I can't just go blundering in. I'll have to tread carefully and actually catch Collum dealing. If I play my cards right, he will be my triumph. He will be the success of my drug campaign. I have no qualms about charging Collum, after all his family are the producers of drugs and he has only himself to blame for his involvement. Besides, they are foreigners and they are 'merde' and they shouldn't be here in the first place.

I have lunch at the pizzeria, then position myself in the best spot for viewing the end of the race. The best part about being a cop is that I can stand anywhere I want and I can move people who are in my way. My uniform gives me power. The race should be nearing its end in about ten minutes.

Many people stop to talk and congratulate me on the success of the drug campaign and it feels great to stand out for the right reasons. Suddenly, there's a loud cheer from further down the street as the front cyclists come into view. The cheering continues for several minutes until the sound changes to cries of dismay. Something is clearly wrong and I begin to run down the street towards the source of the shouting.

When I reach the crowd which has gathered in the street, I see the race has stopped and one of the boys is lying motionless on the road with his discarded cycle by his side.

"What's happened here?" I cry. "Has there been an accident?"

Brigitte, the bar owner steps forward and informs me that the boy simply collapsed onto the road. She tells me he was sweating profusely and he's now unconscious.

"The *pompiers* have been called. They should be here any minute," one man says.

People have rushed forward from the bars and restaurants and some of them are fanning the boy with pieces of cardboard. One man kneels down beside him. He says that he's on holiday here, but he's a doctor from England. He examines the young man as the boy's hysterical mother pleads with him to help her son. The boy's friends are gathered round and the doctor fires questions at them.

"What's he taken?" he asks.

They look at each other then stare at the ground, avoiding the doctor's eyes. I feel a jag of fear. The boy's body is limp and unresponsive.

"Speak to me now," the doctor demands. "I know he's taken something. If I don't know what it is, I might not be able to save him. Do you understand how dangerous this situation is? He may die, if one of you doesn't speak up."

"It was ecstasy. He took ecstasy. The guy who sold it to him said it would give him more energy for a final burst of speed at the end of the race. He was way ahead of us then he just keeled over," one young man says.

The other boys are all talking now. Thank goodness the rest of them were too scared or too broke to buy the drug.

"We must get his temperature down. He is dangerously over-heated," the doctor says. "Fetch a wet towel and all the ice you can find."

I can hear the siren of the *pompier's* vehicle drawing near and I'm relieved, but it will be a few minutes before they get here because of the crowd. I assemble the rest of the cyclists at the side of the road and tell them they cannot leave the area until they've given statements to my officers. They are all white-faced and scared, and rightfully so. One boy steps forward.

"My name is Pierre Montane," he says. "Henri bought the pills from an Irishman. He told us they were safe. I think he said his name was Collum."

"Oh, dear God, no!" I hear an anguished cry and turn to see Aidan O'Brien standing behind me. "What has he done? What has he got himself into? I'll beat the shit out of him when I catch him and I'll kill that feckin' Eddy Albert!"

I manage to grab Aidan before he can take off to carry out his threat, and one of my officers restrains him. The crowd is turning nasty. They're shouting and booing at Aidan. They're clearly blaming him for what has happened. I instruct my officer to remove him from the area before things get out of control and I telephone for backup. I can't get the crowd to disperse as the people are so angry and scared. Within a few minutes, four more officers arrive and I'm very relieved as I've never before felt so alone and exposed.

Finally, the paramedics and the doctor manage to stabilise their patient and they race him off to hospital. The crowd is gradually breaking up and going home and I make my way to

Byron's apartment block to look for Collum. When I arrive at the apartment building, I enter the courtyard through the wrought iron gate and I see Byron sitting on a chair enjoying the sunshine. He's leaning back with his legs stretched in front of him, crossed at the ankles. A cigarette dangles from his thin fingers. His head is tipped back and he has a stylish black hat tilted jauntily over one eye. His long, elegant frame is clad from head to foot in white linen. His fine shirt is almost transparent and his trousers are beautifully tailored. When I draw near he sits up.

"If you're looking for Collum, you're too late, he's been and gone," he says. "But if you're looking for me, your timing is just right. I'm about to have an ice cold beer. Will you join me?"

"It was Collum I came to see, but I will have the beer if you don't mind," I reply.

When we are seated, he tells me that when Collum arrived here he made a call on his mobile phone then dashed into his apartment. Byron saw him, through the open door, gathering some things in a rucksack and within a few minutes he was picked up by a man on a motorbike, and was gone. Back to Spain, no doubt, back to Eddy the Red I think.

I drink my beer and wonder how I'll deal with the fall-out from this incident. If I could have at least charged Collum before he took off, I would've had something to pacify the town. I decide to return to the office before going home and fill out papers formally charging Collum with possession of drugs, just as if I'd arrested him then turned him loose. I'll write on the charge sheet that I found him in possession of a small amount of cannabis, just enough for personal use. After all, he's no longer around to deny it, so it will be his word against mine. If asked, Byron will simply suppose I caught up with the young man after I left here. I'll put the charge sheet and the statements from the cyclists into the file, together with the hospital report on the unconscious boy and my job will be done.

If Collum returns to France I'll pick him up immediately, and if he doesn't, the case will be closed. The charge will come to nothing because I'll have omitted to get his signature on the charge sheet. Oh dear, slapped wrist for me, for the oversight. I can relax now that I have a solution to the problem, so I sit in the sunshine, with my friend, and sip my very cold beer.

Chapter 30

A few days go by and fortunately, the young cyclist is now out of danger but it was touch and go for a while. I'm told it was the quick intervention by the English doctor which helped to bring his temperature down and probably saved his life. Not all English people are work-shy drunks it seems, just the handful who live here – excluding Byron, of course.

I look up from my desk and see Aidan through the window, heading towards my office door. I glance around for somewhere to hide, but I'm too late as he sees me and waves. He opens the door and steps inside.

"I hope you don't mind, Danielle," he says. "I know I don't have an appointment, but I need to speak with you."

I usher him to a chair.

"I went to La Jonquera a couple of days ago to buy supplies," he begins. "Everything is much cheaper there, because it's just over the Spanish border. They buy everything in bulk, so they can pass on the reduced prices."

He pauses for a moment and I wonder if he's actually going to tell me anything, or if he's simply going to make small talk.

"I saw my boy, Danielle," he finally continues. "I saw Collum. He was wearing that ridiculous yellow outfit and I'm ashamed to say that he was selling drugs."

He covers his face with his hands, then draws them down until his chin is resting on his fingertips. He inhales deeply.

"I grabbed the boy and I shouted at him. I asked him what the hell he was doing, getting messed up in this business. I asked why he ran off and why he was working for a scumbag like Eddy. He laughed at me, Danielle. He looked at me and he laughed out loud. I slapped his face, Danielle. God forgive me, but I hit him out of frustration and anger."

Aidan covers his eyes with his hand, his face is red and he's close to tears. I make us both a coffee while he composes himself. He sips it then begins again.

"He shouted at me, 'go on then Dada, hit me, it's all you know how to do'. Then he took a bankroll out of his pocket. It was a huge amount of money, hundreds, perhaps thousands, of euros. 'See this', he said pushing the money into my face, 'this is why I'm here. I'm fed up of being stuck in the middle of nowhere because that's where you and Mammy choose to live. I'm fed up surviving on pocket money and me a grown man. Did you think I could live like that forever?' "

Aidan takes a large linen handkerchief from his trouser pocket and wipes his eyes. His hands shake as he lifts his cup and sips some more coffee.

"I don't know what to do, Danielle. I want him home. I want him to be safe. I want him away from that bloody monster, Eddy. He's using Collum to get at me."

Aidan is clearly distraught and I can understand his fears.

"I hear what you're saying, Aidan," I say, "but unless you give me something to go on, there's nothing I can do to help you. Are you being blackmailed by Eddy, or threatened by him? Do you want to make a statement about it? Because unless you do, I can't touch him. I can ask my friend Paco to try to find Collum. He could have someone arrest him then send him back to France, but then he'll have charges to answer to in Spain. This, of course, might happen anyway if he's caught dealing, although

La Jonquera is a fairly lawless area and his involvement might not even raise an eyebrow there."

"I'd much rather he had a criminal record than he ended up like Jean-Luc," Aidan replies. "Please, do whatever you can to have him arrested. At least he'll be safe then and away from Eddy's influence."

I think for a minute then I say, "I have an idea. I have a charge sheet for the day of the cycle race. I found Collum with a small amount of cannabis in his possession, just enough for him to get a warning not a criminal record. On the strength of that I could call my friend in Spain and ask him to look for Collum. He shouldn't be too hard to find, dressed as he is. I'll ask my friend to do me a favour. Simply pick him up, then meet me at the border. I'll search Collum there. That way, if he is carrying drugs, he'll be charged in France."

I know I'm lying about the charge sheet but Aidan's agreement will make it seem true, and if Collum protests, he'd never be believed over his father and a senior policewoman.

"Bless you, Danielle," Aiden says "That might very well save my boy. Bless you."

We agree on this tactic as a way forward. Aiden stands, gulps down the last of his coffee, shakes my hand then leaves the office. If this works out, I'll have my drug pusher to present to the court and to the town. I rub my hands together in anticipation. It doesn't get much better than this.

Chapter 31

Things don't really settle down after the incident at the cycle race. People are edgy. It's the height of the tourist season, but everybody is suspicious of strangers. The relationship between the locals and the tourists are strained, to say the least. There's been no sign of Collum, either here or in Spain, but I've had reports that the bike rider has been seen talking to groups of teenagers, on more than one occasion. I get the feeling that some people are judging me and finding me lacking. There are rumblings from members of the Commune Committee and even from the Mayor. This is no longer a carefree place to live.

Eddy's black Mercedes has been sighted in town a couple of times, but nobody has actually seen Eddy. He's not welcome in any of the cafes or bars. Aidan and Siobhan are broken people. Aidan blames himself for his son's disappearance and Siobhan blames him too.

Only Patricia and I are happy, and we try not to be too obvious when we're in town. We are sharing so much now that we've become more instinctive about each other's needs and our home life is blissful. We're at home and about to sit down to eat our evening meal when the siren sounds twice. The noise reverberates all over the mountains.

"Something big must have happened," Patricia says. "Do you think that you'll need to go? I've made your favourite '*tarte au fromage*' but I can heat it later if you have to leave."

Before I can answer my mobile rings.

"There are two major fires," the voice on the phone says. "The mountain is on fire on both sides and the *pompiers* have called for help from every town in the region. You might want to liaise with them before heading off."

I scribble down some details, then I hang up the phone. I tell Patricia that I'll have to go and I ask her to pack me a slice of her '*tarte au fromage*' and a couple of large bottles of water in case it becomes an all night job. She does this as I change back into my uniform.

When I leave the house and make for my car, I can smell smoke in the air, and when I look up at the mountain, I can see a red glow in the evening sky coming from the region of the O'Brien's farm. There's another red glow further along, on the opposite side of the mountain, and I think it might be coming from the farm owned by a Spaniard called José Duarte. However, as I think the second fire could be beyond Duarte's farm, and actually over the border in Spain, I make the decision to drive in the direction of the O'Brien's land because I can't be in two places at once.

I drive higher and higher along the mountain road, and as I get nearer to the fire, I can smell the distinctive smell of burning cannabis. When I arrive I'm met by one of the *pompiers* who advises me that a large field has been deliberately set alight.

"There is a fire-break all around the field," he informs me. "Someone has worked very hard to create it so that the whole mountain didn't go up. It's bizarre. The field contained a very valuable crop of cannabis, yet it's been deliberately burned by the owner. He's standing over there, but he hasn't said a word. He's just staring at the flames. I've had a phone call from the men working the other fire and it's exactly the same scenario.

I just don't get it. Maybe you can talk to him and make some sense of it."

I thank the officer and walk over to where Aidan is standing. His ruddy face is shiny and sweaty and streaked with soot. He gives me a sheepish grin and nods at me when I arrive.

"I did it for Collum," he says. If I don't have the drugs, then Eddy can't use him to blackmail me. I've been very careful with the fire, but I had to burn it. You can see that Danielle. Can't you? My son has to come first. I admit I was growing cannabis, so you can arrest me if you like."

I look at the broken man standing beside me and I almost feel sorry for him.

"There's time enough for that, Aidan," I say. "I'll take your statement in the morning. I do hope that you're right and this brings your boy home to you. Where are Siobhan and the children? Are they in the house?"

"No, they're staying with friends," he replies. "I didn't want them involved. I got us into this mess and I'll get us out of it."

"Do you know anything about the other fire?" I ask, "The one over the mountain."

"Yes, it is José Duarte's fields that are burning. His son is also gone. He too, is somewhere in Spain working for Eddy. That bastard has stolen our children and this is the only thing we could think of doing to fight back. We're desperate, Danielle. If the fields are gone, and we're arrested, then he can't use the boys to blackmail us, and just maybe, he'll let them come home."

I wish it were that simple, but Eddy is a vindictive man and this act will probably make him tighten his grip on the boys even more. At least my policing problem is solved as I'll make another two drug-related arrests and become a hero once again. The people of the town will be delighted that two supplies of drugs have been eradicated, due to my sterling police work. I pat Aidan on the back and try to console him. Then I arrange for him to come into the police station tomorrow afternoon, as he'll probably be awake for most of the night. He agrees to get José Duarte to come with him. Then I walk back to my car where I sit and munch on the delicious tart Patricia has packed for me and wash it down with cold water. I'm feeling rather smug. By the end of the day tomorrow, I'll have my arrests and I don't even have to bring them in. They'll come to me. If I play my cards right, a commendation might just be heading my way too.

Chapter 32

My prediction is correct and the whole town is talking about the drug busts and the burning of the fields. But what I didn't anticipate is that it's a double-edged sword. Now everyone wants to hold a special meeting to talk about the drug problem and what more can be done to solve it. They particularly want to discuss Edvard Albert and the bike riding drug pusher, who's still in our town. I'm to be given the honour of being the guest speaker it seems, and I'm also to be presented with an award. Why couldn't they simply give me the award then leave well alone? This town is very good at giving presentations for minor achievements. Even the farmer who grows the heaviest apricot is given an award. Now that they're calling a public meeting, I'm afraid of my shortcomings being highlighted, instead of my achievements.

Patricia is very excited about the meeting because she's been invited to attend with me. She's had a formal invitation from the Mayor and she sees it as an acceptance of us and our living arrangement. I'm not so sure about this and I would much prefer it if she didn't attend, but I can't suggest such a thing or her feelings will be hurt. So she dresses in her best and most classic outfit and she irons my uniform and polishes my shoes, and with some trepidation, we arrive at the Community Centre.

The evening begins with the Mayor presenting me with a certificate of merit for outstanding police work. It's embarrassing, to say the least. Patricia is sitting in the middle of the front row, next to the Mayor's wife, and she's beaming with delight. The Mayor's wife, Marjorie, is wearing a formal black jacket and skirt with a tailored white cotton blouse. The outfit is topped off with a large black hat. Her hair is long and also black, and she has the appearance of a well-dressed, skinny magpie. Patricia applauds enthusiastically, along with everyone else, as I receive the award and her eyes are filled with pride. The Mayor delivers a speech about how much work has been done to achieve this outcome and then invites me to talk about what I intend to do next. I look around the room, at the faces of the people who are waiting expectantly for me to speak, and I'm terrified. What on earth do I tell them?

The room is uncomfortably warm and my uniform makes me hot and sweaty. I'm so nervous that my knees are knocking and my hands are shaking. I stall for time by beginning my talk with thanks to the Commune Committee and the Mayor for my award. Then I go over once again, the work that's been done to achieve the arrests. I remember to praise my junior officers for their help and hard work. I then go on to say that I'm negotiating with Spanish police to bring Collum O'Brien back to France to face charges. This meets with rapturous applause and I breathe a sigh of relief. I also say that my officers and I are working very hard to catch the bike rider, to question him about drug dealing, and we're hopeful this will soon be achieved. There is more rapturous applause. At this point, the Mayor interrupts me and suggests we break for coffee then afterwards, resume the meeting for questions. I can't get off the stage quickly enough and I hope I'm now off the hook.

Patricia is speaking to Marjorie and I go and join them. It's a good decision as it stops anyone else from approaching me and forcing me into a conversation. The three of us are having a chat about the forthcoming artisan market which Marjorie is arranging. Its purpose is to help raise awareness for the work our local artists and craftsmen produce. As it is the tourist season, it will give local people a platform to sell their wares. She thanks me in advance for the work the police will do to enable the stalls to be set up. It's at this point when the Mayor joins us and suggests that we reconvene the meeting, and to my dismay, I find myself being ushered back onto the stage.

From a polite and pleasant start, the meeting descends into bedlam. People are standing up and shouting out questions, all at the same time. They're arguing with each other and with the Mayor, who's trying his best to restore order. The main topic of conversation is Edvard Albert and what the police are going to do about him. Everyone has a story to tell about how he affects their family, and what he represents.

When the people in the crowd realise that nothing will be discussed until they settle down, silence resumes and I have no choice but to run through my standard reply once again. I advise them that unless someone comes forward with hard evidence, or unless we, the police department, actually see Edvard committing a crime and arrest him, there's nothing we can do. It doesn't matter how unpleasant the man is – and we're all agreed that he is a very nasty piece of work – or how much we dislike him being in our town, or how much we suspect him of criminal activities; unless he actually commits a crime, he's free to remain here.

At this point a small group of men stand up and address the meeting. They're all friends and their spokesman, who's the local butcher, says that if the police can't touch Edvard then they'll speak to him themselves and invite him to leave town. He almost sneers at me when he says this, and his attitude is very unsettling. The crowd applauds and everyone talks approvingly. I feel they're encouraging these men to become vigilantes and I must give my opinion and regain control.

"Messieurs," I say, "I understand your frustration and there is no law that says you cannot talk to him. However, I urge you not to lose sight of the fact that he is potentially a very dangerous man with very dangerous associates. If you lay one finger on him, you'll not only be breaking the law, but you may leave yourself open to unimaginable repercussions."

Once again, the meeting descends into bedlam and this time, the Mayor is forced to wind it up. Patricia and I make a hasty departure along with the Mayor and his wife, and when we're outside, he apologises for what has occurred and praises me for keeping my cool and delivering sound advice. As we depart, his wife calls to Patricia. "See you next week," she says.

Patricia and I jump into the car and we head for the peace and quiet of home with Patricia clutching my award and grinning from ear-to-ear.

"Marjorie is coming to the dance class next week," she says. "Imagine that! I might be partnering the Mayor's wife if we're as short of men as we usually are. We're accepted, Danielle. If the Mayor's wife accepts us, then everyone else will too."

I don't want to burst her bubble because she's so happy, but I have my doubts. I fear we'll never be accepted in the way she wants us to be. This town is too locked in tradition and they will always see our living arrangement as something more sordid than it actually is.

Chapter 33

Patricia has been preparing for the artisan market by producing paintings. She is rather a skilled artist and, although her work is simple and easy for her to produce, it's colourful and very appealing. As is usual in this region, her paintings carry a hefty price tag, with the smallest of her works priced at one hundred euros, ranging up to three hundred euros for the largest canvas. She's produced fourteen works of art, which she hopes to sell to the tourists.

I'm constantly amazed at the high prices artists charge for what's usually very little work, but I can't say anything to Patricia or I'll not be popular, to say the least. She is desperately trying to find ways of making money so she can give up her job, and I do everything in my power to encourage her. She feels that working in the funeral parlour has lost its charm, if ever it had any, and she finds dealing with the bereaved depressing and exhausting.

Since I was promoted we have more money coming in, and after the incident with Patricia's 'date' Claire, we've decided to pool our resources. I've paid for the framing materials for Patricia's artwork and I've built the frames for her. If she sells anything, the money will go into our new joint bank account. Although the jams and pies she produces bring in a profit, it's not enough to allow her to give up her full time job.

The Mayor's wife, Marjorie, has become Patricia's new best friend and she's confided in Patricia that her brother, who lives in Paris, is gay. This information explains a lot to me about why she's being so kind to us. She asks Patricia to keep her secret and I can understand why, as the people of this town are very bigoted. Marjorie says it's a relief to be able to talk about her beloved younger brother without the fear of gossip or rejection.

Before we know it, the day of the market comes around and I find myself once again packing up my car with Patricia's wares and a very excitable Ollee. When we arrive, we find that Marjorie has allocated the best pitch in the market to Patricia and we are delighted. I leave her to set up and I move the car into a reserved parking space. I've decided to have this market policed, because with the angry feelings about the drug situation that were voiced at the meeting, I feel a strong police presence is essential. Besides, with the large number of people visiting the market, we might find one or two undesirables amongst the crowds. We have a couple of homeless people residing in and around town. They refuse to move into apartments because they prefer to sleep outside with their dogs, but I'm sure they'll feel differently when winter comes. They have a tendency to get drunk at events such as this and then they annoy the tourists by begging.

I've been liaising with colleagues in nearby Ceret and I'm not surprised to discover the bike rider, suspected of drug pushing, has been seen there too. They're desperate to get their hands on him, but although they've managed to intercept him once, he had time to dispose of any drugs he was carrying and they were forced to release him without charge. They've also seen Edvard's car in town and often on the same day the bike rider has been there.

I keep popping back and forward between Patricia's stall and my colleagues and everything is under control. By lunchtime, Patricia has sold two paintings and I'm amazed and delighted.

She has sold both the cheapest and the most expensive of her pictures, one of them to a tourist from England, and one of them to a man from Bezier. When she tells me this and shows me the cash she's been paid, she becomes very emotional. I place my arm around her shoulders and give her a hug and she doesn't quite know whether to laugh or cry. I'm really surprised she's been paid in cash, as it seems rather a lot of money for some-one to carry around a market, but one of the other stall holders assures me this is quite usual.

By four o'clock, Patricia is beginning to pack up. She's sold another one of her cheaper paintings and taken a deposit on a fourth, which is to be collected next week. She's had an aston-ishing day. I'm thrilled for her because she has five hundred and twenty euros and another hundred euros due when the painting is picked up. She would have to work for nearly three weeks to earn that kind of money. The icing on the cake is that she's also had an enquiry from an art dealer in Perpignan.

I'm about to tell my colleagues to knock off early as the mar-ket is coming to an end, when there's a commotion near the fast food van. One of the young policemen has grabbed the bike rider, who is struggling to escape. I run to help my colleague, and between us, we manage to wrestle the biker to the ground. He is kicking and punching at us and he manages to catch my col-league with a powerful kick to the stomach, which both floors and winds him, and causes him to loosen his grip. I'm in real danger of being unable to hang on to the man by myself and I'm relieved when the owner of the fast food van appears and helps me by sitting astride him.

My colleague recovers from the kick and returns to help me. When we remove the man's helmet, we are surprised to see that he is only about twenty years of age. When I search him, I find cannabis, ecstasy and even some cocaine. It's a fantastic result. As we march him off to the police station, people in the crowd begin to applaud and I can't help smiling.

We discover that he's Spanish, but he won't tell us any more, other than his name and an address in La Jonquera. When I ask him if he knows Edvard Albert, he clams up. All I can do is charge him and then call my colleagues from Ceret to pick him up, as we have no facilities here to hold him.

The two officers who are working for me at the moment, agree to stay with the young man until he's collected. They will also prepare the paperwork because I must now leave to go and pick up Patricia and Ollee. As I head out of the office, I punch the air with delight.

Chapter 34

It's late morning on a beautiful, sunny Saturday and I'm sitting outside the café with Byron enjoying a rich, milky coffee and a warm '*pain au chocolate*'. I have the day off and Patricia is due to finish work at lunchtime, when she'll meet me here. She has an appointment in Perpignan with the owner of an art gallery, to discuss whether or not he'll include her work for sale in his establishment and I'm going to drive her. I don't much fancy driving in the centre of Perpignan on a Saturday afternoon in high summer, and parking will be impossible, but I have to support her, and who knows, this might be the very opportunity she's been waiting for. Byron and I have just been discussing how quiet it is here this morning.

"It's as if all the tourists have suddenly been whisked off into space," I comment.

"Or Perpignan," he replies with a wicked grin.

"Very funny."

"Oh dear, here comes trouble," he says.

I turn my head in the direction that he's looking, to see Eddy's distinctive car park almost immediately in front of us. Within a couple of minutes Aidan O'Brien's old truck pulls up behind it. They don't seem to notice me sitting where I am and Byron and I watch as both parties climb out of their vehicles. Eddy leans luxuriantly against his car and his driver stands almost to attention beside him, with his black gloved hands clasped in front of him. Aidan and Siobhan walk forward to join them. Aidan's ruddy face looks troubled and Siobhan's teeth are gritted with determination as they approach Eddy.

"I believe that you wanted to see me, Mr. O'Brien," Eddy says. He has not stood up straight but is still leaning against his car with his lips stretched into a benign smile. "I assume you want to apologise for your atrocious behaviour."

I can hear every word that's being said and I quickly confirm with Byron that he too, can hear the conversation in case one of them says something incriminating.

"Apologise? Me?" Aiden replies with an incredulous tone in his voice.

"My husband has nothing to apologise for," Siobhan cuts in. Her Irish accent is very pronounced and she's unable to control her anger.

"If you believe that then we have nothing more to discuss," Eddy replies and stands up to leave.

"I want to talk about my boy," Aidan shouts and he reaches out to grab hold of Eddy. Eddy's driver leans over and stays his hand, removing it from Eddy's arm.

"I don't know what you're talking about," Eddy says. "Why would I want to say anything to you about Collum?" He pauses for a moment and his eyes are hard and cold. "Well," he continues, "if you insist. I must say that he is a fine boy and a hard worker. It's just a pity about his drug problem. I don't suppose you'll ever see him again," he adds maliciously.

Eddy grins at them and makes to open the door of the car to leave, and that's when all hell breaks loose. Siobhan flies at Eddy, screaming like a banshee. She jumps onto his back, she has one arm around his throat and she's clawing at his face with her other hand. As the driver steps in to help Eddy, Aidan throws hard, swinging punches at him and manages to catch him square on the chin. Although he's not a particularly skilled fighter, he's a stocky built, heavy-set man. Aidan lands a second punch, one that Muhammad Ali would have been proud of. The driver is semi-conscious before he hits the ground.

I jump to my feet and look at Byron; I'm alarmed. He grasps my arm and pulls me back into my seat.

"I'm off duty," I say, "but what should I do?"

His reply is a shrug and a smile. This Englishman has mastered this very French mannerism to perfection.

"Perhaps one of us should phone for the police," he replies, then he shrugs again. "Oh, sod it," he continues, "let someone else phone it in. Neither of us really wants to get involved – besides, Siobhan seems to be winning."

So we sit in the sunshine and continue enjoying our refreshments as we watch the rest of the floorshow. Eventually a police car pulls up and the officers break up the fight. I'm delighted when they have to call for an ambulance as both Eddy and his driver require treatment. At last, the tables have been turned and Eddy is the injured party. Maybe this will deter him from coming back to our town.

Chapter 35

When Patricia joins me, I take my leave of Byron and we get into my car and head for Perpignan. As expected, driving in the town is hell. I find the gallery easily enough, but as luck would have it, it's in one of the busiest parts of town. By the time I've driven past it three times and still found nowhere to park, Patricia is beginning to panic about being late for her appointment. I'm feeling agitated and end up parking immediately in front of the gallery, in a tow-away zone. I'll just have to keep my eye on the car and if a police officer comes along, show my badge and say that I'm on official business.

When we enter the gallery, I see that although it has a rather small shop front, it's like the 'Tardis' from Dr. Who. It stretches into quite an enormous space which houses dozens of paintings, sculptures and unique pieces of furniture. The gallery owner greets us and I'm invited to look around while he and Patricia talk. I see him guide her to an elegant antique sideboard, which is positioned against a wall, and she takes the photographs of her paintings from her bag and lays them out for him to peruse.

I'm trying not to stare at them, but I'm anxious for her. She would love to see her work displayed here as it would be her first real step toward becoming a professional artist. After about twenty minutes I'm bored, but Patricia and the gallery owner are still chatting and discussing her work so I excuse myself and go outside to get some fresh air and check on the car. The street is full of traffic, people rushing around, and noise and dust. It's quite unpleasant, so I'm relieved when Patricia finally joins me and we sit in the car to talk.

She tells me that the gallery owner liked her work and he's agreed to display two of her paintings, on a sale or return basis, for one month. If they sell in that time, he'll give her a regular spot in the gallery and will always carry at least two of her works. I don't know what I expected, but she seems delighted with this offer and I'm delighted for her. The hustle and bustle of Perpignan makes me realise just how lucky we are to live where we do and, after a very eventful day, we're happy to arrive home and eat our evening meal in the garden.

We spend a quiet Sunday together, and apart from going for a walk in the mountains to gather blackberries, we do little more than loll about the house. When I arrive at the office on Monday morning, I'm well rested and ready to work.

My colleague greets me, pours me a cup of coffee, then he tells me that Eddy has been treated at the hospital for a broken nose, two black eyes, and given stitches for injuries to both his mouth and his ear. His driver has a mild concussion. I'm informed that neither of the O'Briens suffered any injury and they're both claiming they acted in self-defence. I'm asked to give an opinion about whether or not to charge them with assault.

I ask my colleague to consider the fact that Eddy and his driver are gangsters, who are big and very strong. Aidan, on the other hand, is a fat, middle aged man and his wife is a woman of average build. Further, it seems that Eddy and his driver discharged themselves from hospital against medical advice, and both they and their car have now gone.

"Why give yourself extra work?" I say. "Just write it up as a minor incident. Put a note in the file stating verbal warnings were given and then the matter is closed. I don't think either of the parties involved will want to take it further."

He's happy to agree with me as, like me, he doesn't want to deal with Eddy unless he has absolutely no choice. I leave the office and take a walk into the town centre as I'm anxious to see how people are reacting to these recent events. I haven't walked very far before I see posters showing a picture of Eddy being loaded into an ambulance, under the heading, 'Say No to Drugs', displayed on railings and in shop windows. Somebody has obviously taken great delight in photographing the event, which they've turned into posters. I chuckle every time I see the picture and I wonder if Eddy has seen it yet, because I'm sure that if he has, he won't find it so amusing.

Chapter 36

Two weeks pass, then three, and there has been no sign of Eddy in town. He's still licking his wounds; I think to myself. The young bike rider was charged and then released by the police in Ceret. He'll appear in court in due course, if he doesn't do a runner. He's admitted to drug offences and he also said he worked for Edvard Albert, but only in the capacity of delivery driver. Unfortunately, he didn't implicate Eddy in the drugs charge.

There has been a subtle change in the region and summer has become autumn. The tourists have nearly all gone home and the town is peaceful once again. The local businesses have had a fairly good year and their efforts have allowed them to bank money for the quiet winter months ahead. The fierceness has gone out of the sun and it has become mellow and soft, like thick golden syrup. The trees on the mountains are a rich hue of reds, yellows and oranges and the sky is a vivid turquoise blue.

Today is market day and my darling Patricia has once again filled a stall with her produce. There's been no word yet from the gallery about her paintings and she's beginning to think that perhaps they won't sell, but it hasn't deterred her. Today she's selling jams and chutneys and they are flying out. She's also placed a folder with photographs of her paintings on the stall, in the hope of striking up interest in them. I've worked out our finances and I plan to tell her today, we can afford for her to reduce the hours she works in the funeral parlour, to give her more time for her own business. I know she'll be delighted and although there'll be a bit less money for extras, I want to do this for her.

We've begun to get our house and garden in order for the winter. Patricia has plenty of bottles and jars of her produce in the larder and our freezer is filled with rich stews and soups. I've done some work on the chicken house so Patricia's 'children' are warm, safe and comfortable, and I've cleared out areas in the garden to be ready for next year's planting. Although the winter can be very cold, it's usually dry, so we're rarely restricted to the house. I love the feeling I get inside as we plan for the dark nights ahead. Our home has become a haven for us. I delight in the preparations we're making and every piece of work we do enriches my soul.

The local children have settled back into school and nobody has complained to me about drugs. I don't believe the problem has gone, as there are still growers in the mountains, but at least it has sunk below the surface again and I'm out of the spotlight. I hope Eddy won't return to this area, but if he does, I hope that he'll not appear in town because it's his presence which unsettles folk.

As I walk around the market, I buy the items on the shopping list Patricia has given me. I see Marjorie, the Mayor's wife, is standing beside the *savonnier's* stall, she's endeavouring to help Henriette, the stall holder, explain to an English woman that the soap which is stamped with the word 'opium', has nothing to do with drugs. It is simply the name of the scent, like rose, or jasmine.

Marjorie greets me with a hug and a kiss on both cheeks then tells me excitedly that Patricia is to be given a commission. She'll be asked to produce a painting of the town, to be presented to her husband by the Commune Committee. Marjorie is delighted, both for her husband and for Patricia. She says that I mustn't say a word to Patricia because it is Monsieur Bonet who should commission the work, as he is the representative of the Committee. However, I'm told that he'll be telephoning her this evening and the budget for the painting is three hundred euros. I'm so thrilled for Patricia and I decide to tell her that she can reduce her hours of work before Monsieur Bonet telephones, so as not to dilute the gesture I'm making.

The market is winding up and I put the produce I've bought into the car and go to help Patricia pack up her table. She's sold out of all of the jams and chutneys and she excitedly tells me that a couple from Perpinan visited her stall. They told her they've seen her paintings in the gallery and are considering a purchase. I love to see Patricia so happy.

However, just when I think this is going to be a perfect day, something dreadful happens. There are two men whose responsibility it is to clear up and clean up after the market. They are simple men who've been given this position to ensure they have work and they take pride in the job they do. The area is always spotless when they're finished. Through the week, they also clean up after the daily produce market.

They've wheeled the heavy bin into the centre of the market area in order to fill it with rubbish, when one of them makes a gruesome discovery. As he opens the bin lid, he can see something which terrifies him. He's so shocked, he cannot contain his distress. He's screaming and shouting and flapping his hands as he runs around and around in ever-increasing circles. This frightens his work mate, who drops to the ground and hugs his knees. He shapes his body into a tight ball and rocks back and forth, moaning and crying. With no real choice in the matter and suffering much trepidation, I go to their assistance.

When I look into the bin I can see that a body is rolled up, with the knees bent. I can see the back and one arm, but the rest of the body is hidden from view. With the help of three of the male stallholders, the bin is tipped over and the body unrolls onto the road. There's a lot of congealed blood pooled in the bottom of the bin, and the face of the corpse especially, is covered in blood. The right hand has been severed and it remains in the bottom of the bin. It's a sickening sight and one of my helpers runs off, retching. It takes me only a few moments to realise that I'm looking at the body of the young bike rider. I immediately call for assistance and it's not long before all of the services arrive. For once, Dr. Poullet is first on the scene as he lives close by.

"Hello again, Officer," he addresses me then he looks at the body. After a few minutes he says "Mmm, this is an easy one. It is definitely murder and it is ritualistic. Very nasty."

"What do you mean by ritualistic?" I question. "Like devil worship or witchcraft?"

He looks at me with an expression on his face that's usually reserved for children who ask stupid questions, and I'm immediately embarrassed.

"Ritualistic as in gang-related like the Mafia," he says. "Look at the face, the tongue has been cut out and the right hand has also been severed. It looks to me as if someone wanted to give a very clear message. This young man obviously upset some very dangerous people."

I immediately think of Edvard Albert. He's the kind of man who could have had this terrible murder committed and this young man did mention him to the police. Maybe that's why his tongue has been cut out. In some countries, the cutting off of a hand is a punishment for thieves and this man was found with drugs and money that were later confiscated.

I'm really unnerved. It's a ghastly crime and I can't help dwelling on the fact that this body is someone's son. Some poor soul is going to have to identify a beloved son in this mutilated condition. I'm very frightened by the whole business and I wouldn't want to face Eddy any time soon. In fact, if I saw him now, I would walk the other way.

Finally, the doctor is finished with the preliminary examination and the corpse is removed for further study. The bin is taken away on a truck, as it too must be examined. The two men who discovered the body have been taken to hospital to be treated for shock and I'm left at the crime scene with two other officers. They agree to set up a table at the market place as an incident area, so anyone who thinks they might have seen something can come forward and give a statement. However, I don't hold out much hope of gathering information, as anyone who has seen something will keep their mouth shut, and wisely so. After seeing what happened to Jean- Luc and now this young man, only a fool would come forward.

I go to the office and send a brief email to Detective Gerard, outlining what has occurred. I'll not ask him for help, but I sincerely hope he offers some as I'm way out of my depth. I'm in a sombre mood as I drive home with Patricia and Ollee, and I'm very disappointed that our special day has been spoiled.

Chapter 37

News of the murder spreads like wildfire. Everyone is talking about it and everyone is scared. The last few weeks have been like a rollercoaster ride, with my emotions changing with every rise and fall. A cloud of suspicion hangs over the whole region and nobody is free of it. Neighbour suspects neighbour, friends suspect friends, brother suspects brother, everyone is scared that someone they know is involved. Our town is like a ghost town in the evenings as parents place curfews on their children.

There's a rising wave of anger amongst some of the most outspoken men in the community. These are men who do not back down when they get frightened; on the contrary, they get more aggressive. If they were a pack of wild dogs, they would be the biggest dogs, the leaders. Not surprisingly, two of these men are on the Commune Committee. They're calling for action and they are beginning to get support. Against all my advice, they've formed a small group with three others. They intend to 'police' certain areas to free up the real police for more important things like catching the murderer.

This is a blatant vigilante group and I advise them they have no power within the law, and in some instances, they might actually break the law themselves. It is to no avail. I'm paid lip-service, but they still intend to go ahead with their group nevertheless. I try to enlist the help of Marjorie, by asking her to get her husband to talk some sense into these men, but she tells me that the Mayor is in agreement with them. She says that the people of the town are happy with me and with the results I've achieved, but it's not enough. They still feel trapped by the gangsters, and the drug problem has spread like a cancer and is threatening to kill the way of life we all love so much.

So with no other choice, I call my colleagues to a meeting in my office, to try to work out a strategy for dealing with the vigilantes. These people are decent, courageous and prominent members of our society, but we cannot let them break the law, neither can we stop them from taking action it seems. I suggest a softly, softly approach at all times. I further suggest that we are respectful, but careful not to condone anything that causes them to step out of line. My colleagues are moaning at me. They say our job is hard enough at the moment without having to pussy-foot around a group of well-meaning busybodies, and they're right. However, I remind them that the Mayor and the Commune Committee hold all the power in our town and, as such, we're stuck with them.

We're all feeling rather despondent and de-motivated, and we're deep in our own thoughts when the ringing telephone forces us to get back to work. I answer the phone and a voice, one that I don't recognise, tells me about a man who lives just within my jurisdiction. The voice says that this man is growing cannabis for Eddy the Red and he demands that I arrest him and destroy his crop, before it's too late. I ask to whom I am speaking but I'm met with silence, then he hangs up.

At first, I'm not sure whether or not it's just a crank call, but the more I think about it, the more I believe it to be true. I decide to investigate by sending one of my colleagues to the area to see if any cannabis is, in fact, growing there. I've told him not to do anything if it is, but simply to assess the situation then stay out of sight and telephone me. If anything is found, I want to be the one who makes the arrest. It will take him at least an hour to get to the area so I leave the office and go for a walk by the river to clear my head.

I sit on a bench at the riverside and watch the ducks as they swim back and forth and around and around in the sunshine and I envy their simple existence. Then I remember that one day, they might very well become somebody's dinner and I realise that life is never simple. I'm feeling rather morose and philosophical, and if I'm honest, a bit sorry for myself, when my mobile rings and I answer it.

"Danielle, it's me, Patricia. Can you talk just now?"

"Hello Patricia, yes," I reply. "What's up?"

"I've just had great news! The gallery telephoned me and one of my paintings is sold and the other has been reserved. They want me to bring in three more pictures, three this time, Danielle. Isn't that fantastic?"

Her excitement and her news give my spirits a well needed boost and helps me to put things into perspective. I tell Patricia I'm thrilled for her and we must celebrate, and I suggest that I take her out for dinner tonight.

"Put on your best clothes," I say, "because we're going somewhere posh and expensive. After all, it's not every day I get to be seen out with a professional artist."

She squeals with delight at my suggestion and I still hear the sound of her laughter in my head, long after she hangs up the phone. I walk back to the office feeling a bit happier, and when I enter, the young policeman who I left to man the office, informs me there's been a call. The other officer has arrived at the area which was reported to us and he confirms there is cannabis being grown there. He's observed two men working in the field and he thinks they're the only people around.

I immediately telephone him back, tell him to stay where he is, and say we're coming to assist him, then I lock up the office and we head for my car. It seems to take forever to drive to the site, but then a journey always seems longer when you're in a hurry. When we arrive, we rendezvous with the other officer and all three of us approach the farm.

As soon as the two men see us coming, they put up their hands and hang their heads. They offer us no resistance. In fact, they appear to be relieved that we've discovered them, and I'm beginning to wonder if one of them might have been the anonymous caller. I inform them of their rights and they happily climb into my car to be driven to town and formally charged.

"We couldn't see a way out of this mess, Officer," the older man says. "We're relieved that it's over."

"Why didn't you just burn your crop?" I ask. "You could have planted something else on your land."

"And end up like Jean-Luc?" he answers, "No, thank you, we prefer to stay alive."

"Will you testify against the person who forced you into this position?"

"Again, no thank you, Officer, we saw what happened to the young man in the wheelie bin. We take full responsibility for our actions and we'll be happy when you destroy our crop. Even though we're desperately short of money, we'd rather be broke than dead."

We formally charge the pair and we discover that they're brothers who are local to the region. By the end of the day, we've received yet another anonymous call about a grower and I'm now fairly certain that these people are turning themselves in. The arrests are certainly doing my career no harm and maybe this is the only way to ever be free from Eddy.

Chapter 38

The dead bike rider turns out to be a twenty-year-old runaway from Carcassonne, named Franck Boyer. I interview his heart-broken parents shortly after they identify his body, and I'm moved by their deep sadness. They'd tried everything they could think of to locate the young man after he left home, aged just sixteen, but to no avail. They are still mystified about what went wrong with their son that would cause him to run off in the first place.

The Boyers are a respectable, middle class couple. He works as a bank manager and she volunteers at a hospice. They have three other children, all older than Franck. He was their baby. Madame Boyer tells me proudly that all their children are clever and have good jobs and Franck was clever too. He got good grades, never missed school, and he was never in any trouble. The change in him seemed to occur just before the Christmas school break, four years ago. Monsieur Boyer tells me that his son became quiet and uncommunicative and he would disappear on his bike for hours at a time. Then one day, he simply didn't return. They searched everywhere for him and they even hired a detective, but he could not be found. I ask them if he could have been taking drugs.

"Maybe," Monsieur Boyer replies, "but we wouldn't have known as we had no experience of drugs and we wouldn't have suspected it of our son. Why would we?"

Madame Boyer takes a tissue from the handbag she's clutching and she removes her spectacles and gently dries her eyes. I look at the respectable couple in front of me and I feel terrible about having to interview them. They are gentle, gracious people and this is the worst day of their lives.

"There is one thing I noticed," Madame Boyer cuts in. "Not long before that Christmas break, Franck would leave for school happy and chatty as normal, but when he returned, he was quiet and unresponsive. This was happening nearly every day. I thought that maybe he'd fallen out with one of his friends. Do you think he could have been given drugs at the school?"

"That was probably the case," I reply. "We're experiencing some incidents of school-aged teenagers being sold drugs, and it's becoming a real problem."

"You must make it stop, Officer, I beg you," Madame says. "You must search the school. No other parent should have to experience what we've gone through. No other parent should have to lose their baby."

She hangs her head and shields her eyes with her hand, and with the other hand, she gently mops up her tears. I feel cruel to be asking questions that upset them so, but I have one more thing to ask, then I can leave them alone with their grief. I mention the name Edvard Albert to them, but I'm disappointed when they tell me they've never heard of him.

I'm all fired up after my meeting with the Boyers. It was something she said that spurred me into action. I telephone Marjorie, as she's on the School Board, and I arrange for her to call a parents meeting. I ask her to send every child home with a letter, requesting that at least one parent or guardian from every family attend. It's time to tackle the problem at a grass roots level. I tell my colleagues that they must all attend the meeting and

I draft in help from other officers as well. I'm planning a major assault on the pushers and it will begin in two days' time.

...

The day of the meeting is upon us and I feel nervous, but exhilarated as well. I've planned exactly what will occur and I'm prepared for any outcome. When we arrive, I place my fellow officers at the doorway of the school hall because I don't want anyone to leave until I'm ready. Then I climb onto the stage and begin my talk. I start with a recount of what's happened to Franck Boyer and how it has affected his grieving parents. Every person in the room is silent and listening intently. I tell them he was a good pupil at school and a loving son from a loving family and that his family did everything humanly possible to find their son and bring him home. I tell them of the Boyers' terrible feelings of hopelessness and loss when they were faced with identifying their son's body. I notice some of the mothers in the crowd are wiping away tears and I'm pleased because that's the sort of response I want.

Then I drop the bombshell. I advise the gathering that my officers will take each one of them in turn, accompanied by a teacher, to search their children's lockers. I mention Madame Boyer's insistence that parents should be made aware of any drug problems as they arise and not after it is too late to do anything about it. I explain there will be no official warnings or charges placed on their children's records if drugs are found and each locker will be opened in private, so as not to alert anyone else to the problem. I have screens provided that will be placed around the lockers so several may be searched at once. Anyone whose child has drugs discovered in their locker will be invited to attend a private interview with their child later in the week. These interviews will be held discreetly, either in the school, or at their home.

There is a rumble of talking but no outbursts or complaints. If anything, there's a feeling of relief that some action is being taken and so we begin the search. Our school is small, there are only about sixty pupils and most of the lockers are emptied on a daily basis so the search takes little time. By the end of the search we've found a small quantity of drugs in three lockers, just enough for personal consumption. However, one locker turns up the jackpot, as hidden in a lunch box, are enough drugs to supply the whole school. The locker belongs to the son of one of the vigilantes and he is enraged by the find. Christian Lesecq is not angry at his son, or indeed the school or even the police. He is enraged to think that the person responsible is Edvard Albert and we have nothing on him. He's frightened that if his son makes a statement implicating Edvard, then he too might incur the same risk and fate as Franck Boyer.

I arrange to meet with him at his home the next evening. I'm sure his son will give me no useful information and I'm worried that Monsieur Lesecq will try to take matters into his own hands. I'm especially concerned as I later discover that one of the other lockers containing drugs is owned by the son of another vigilante.

Although it is now rather late, after the meeting ends and everyone disperses, I return to my office and send another report to Detective Gerard. I'm still hopeful he'll visit and offer me some assistance.

Chapter 39

The Lesecq boy cannot, or will not, tell me very much. According to him, the drugs were supplied by Franck Boyer and he was just holding them because Franck couldn't enter the school. He didn't admit to selling them or even distributing them. In fact, if Charles Lesecq is to be believed, he didn't even use drugs, he simply allowed his locker to be a storage unit for a short time and a small fee. I knew he was lying and his father knew he was lying, but short of beating the truth out of him, there was nothing more to be said.

When I arrive at the office the next morning there's an email from Detective Gerard, inviting me to have lunch with him. He praises me for the results I'm getting and he says that he'll meet me in the café at one o'clock if it's convenient. I immediately email back and accept his offer. I sincerely hope I'm to be offered more than lunch. I've tackled the cannabis growers and the drug problem at the school, as well as investigating two murders and a missing person without help, so it's about time I had some input from him. There's quite a difference between being trusted to work independently and being left out on a limb.

I can't settle in the office knowing I have the meeting at one, so I go to the café at eleven o'clock in the hope of meeting Byron there for a coffee and a chat. He's usually around at that time, and when I arrive, I see I'm not to be disappointed as he's sitting just inside the door reading his morning paper.

"Bonjour, my dear lady," he says as I approach. "How is my favourite officer of the law today?"

He stands and takes my hand and kisses it, before holding a chair out for me. Then he signals to Roland, the proprietor to bring me a coffee. Roland is a big man with a serious face and he's also one of the vigilantes. When he serves my coffee he seems embarrassed about his involvement with the group, as he can't look me in the eye. Byron and I spend a pleasant half hour chatting about this and that, being careful not to mention anything about drugs. I'm tired of everything being about drugs and I wish this town would go back to the way it was before Magda Gold arrived and brought her gangster friends with her.

I feel relaxed talking to Byron, he's intelligent and kind and he always gives me confidence and good advice. He is very amusing and often has me laughing out loud at something he's said. I tell him about Patricia and her success with her painting, and that she's going onto part-time hours from next week, so she can spend more time on her own business. He's delighted and he asks me to congratulate her.

We're having a very pleasant and relaxing interlude when both of us see something that we'd rather not see. Parked across the road is a familiar black Mercedes car and Eddy is climbing out of it, accompanied by his driver and Magda Gold. They're making their way towards the café and I'm surprised, because Roland has made Eddy very unwelcome in the past; he has even refused to serve him.

They sit themselves at an outside table but nobody goes to take their order. Eventually, Eddy stands up and walks to the doorway. His face is still bearing the scars from Siobhan's attack. I can see he's annoyed at not yet being served, as his face is like thunder and his cheek is twitching with anger.

"Three black coffees," he shouts at Roland. "Make it quick, we haven't got all day," then he returns to his companions.

Roland draws himself up to his full height and makes his way to Eddy's table. I can see by the obstinate look on his face that Eddy's going to be turned away, and I'm ready to step in and assist Roland, if he's given any trouble.

"You," he says leaning over Eddy and pointing his finger close to his face, "get off of my chair and get out of my café and take that whore and your trained monkey with you."

Eddy, his face stiff with rage, doesn't blink. He repeats, "Three black coffees. Make it quick, we haven't got all day, and apologise to the lady or I'll make you apologise."

"She was never a lady she's not even much of a whore. She's a diseased little tramp, perfect for the likes of you," Roland says, raising his voice so that all can hear.

I see that Roland has now been joined by two more of the vigilantes. They seem to have come out of nowhere. This situation could escalate very quickly, so I jump up from my chair and go to intervene.

"Monsieur Albert," I say as I step between the vigilantes, "you have been invited to leave and I think you would be wise to do so."

Eddy realises he's outnumbered, so with great reluctance, he and his companions get up to leave. As he stands he pushes over his chair in temper.

"Don't think this is over," he hisses at Roland. "I won't be treated this way by the likes of you. You'll be sorry."

"I don't think so," Roland replies, shaking his head and his friends shake their heads in agreement. Eddy storms off with the sound of their laughter and jeering following him across the street.

I go back to my seat and Byron makes a comment that at least life is not dull.

"I wish it were," I reply. "Right now, I would be delighted to go back to life being dull, it beats dangerous every time."

We chat for another ten minutes, then Byron leaves to do some work. Detective Gerard arrives early and we have an enjoyable lunch. He spends the entire time singing my praises and he tells me that he's commended my work in his monthly report. He also assures me he's available whenever I need him, but offers me no direct help. After all the glowing things he says about me, I feel reluctant to ask for assistance, but I'm sure that was his plan from the outset. When he leaves I feel rather deflated, because once again I'm not sure what to do next.

Chapter 40

When I arrive home after work, I see Patricia has a huge pan of green tomato pickle cooking on the stove. The familiar sweet and sour, sugar and vinegar smell greets me at the door, and when I enter the kitchen, I see that Ollee has been given a marrow bone to gnaw on. The little dog wags his tail happily at me as he works away at the marrow with his tongue, while holding the bone between his front paws. Patricia is working on her painting for the Mayor but she stops when I go to get washed and changed out of my uniform. When I re-enter the kitchen, she serves our evening meal.

All the frustrations of the day disappear when I'm seated at the table eating her delicious food and listening to her excited chatter about what she's been doing today. I wish that neither of us had to work for anyone else, but instead could live our lives doing the things we enjoy. I used to love my job, but that was when I was little more than a traffic cop and there was no crime to speak of in my town.

Everything changed with the arrival of Magda Gold, because she brought Eddy to our town and now it's difficult to get rid of him. It's hard to believe that in the last few short months we've had so much crime committed. Our lives here have become like a Hollywood movie and people are very frightened. Change is not easily embraced at the best of times, and now that everything has changed for the worse, we expect trouble and trauma on a daily basis and it's horrible.

Patricia asks me about my day and I tell her about my disappointing meeting with Detective Gerard. I also tell her about the commotion at the café and she finds it highly amusing, particularly the part when Roland called Magda a diseased little tramp. The conversation inevitably becomes a discussion about the drug problem and she begins to tell me about her colleague Claude's aunt. It seems that she's a lady in her late sixties who unfortunately suffers from multiple sclerosis. Claude has explained to Patricia that his aunt Eveline is a regular cannabis user as it's the only thing that relieves her pain. She also supplies two other sufferers in Perpignan who don't have the facilities to grow the drug for themselves and who are too frightened to buy it from a dealer. Patricia tells me about a very small network of people with MS who've formed a self-help group and have been using cannabis for many years. Most of the group have found it very helpful.

"Claude's aunt Eveline is very frightened now, what with all the problems in town with drugs," Patricia says.

"Why should she be worried more than anyone else?" I ask. "Her supply won't dry up when the farmers stop producing cannabis, as she grows her own."

"That's why she's worried, Danielle. She's frightened you'll charge her as a grower or a dealer because she supplies the drug to two other people."

"That's ridiculous; I'm after the farmers and the peddlers, not old ladies who are ill. In fact, the only person I'm really after is Edvard Albert, because if he were gone, all our problems would leave with him."

"I'll say that to Claude, he'll be so relieved. I just hope his aunt believes him when he tells her everything's okay. She feels very vulnerable right now."

"We all do Patricia. Ask Claude to get his aunt to supply me with the names of the people in her group. I'll ensure there's a note in the file, saying they've to be left alone. That should reassure her."

Patricia thanks me then the conversation changes to her business ventures. She points to the bubbling pot on the stove and tells me that it contains twenty-four euros' profit.

"I've stopped thinking in jars and pies or even paintings" she says. "Now I think only in profit margins. I'm making around eighty euros a week net profit from pies and jars and that's consistent. On exceptional weeks, I can double it without much more effort," she adds proudly. "The only restriction I have is time. I've been canvassing shops in my spare time, and if I wasn't working at the funeral parlour, I could immediately get enough orders to cover three quarters of my wages and I haven't approached hotels or restaurants yet with my pies."

"That's fantastic," I say. "Why don't you give up your job at the funeral parlour? Why work for someone else doing something you hate, when you can have your own business doing something you love? If you can cover three quarters of your wages with baking and cooking, you don't need to sell many paintings to make up the difference."

"I'd only need to sell eight in a year," she replies. "If I sell more, then I'm well into profit. I've already sold six paintings in two months between the market, the gallery and the commission I'm working on for the Mayor."

"I'm so proud of you, Patricia," I say. "I always knew you could do it."

"It's because you believe in me. Without you, I'd be working in the funeral parlour until I became a client instead of an employee. When you helped me to go part-time, I realised I could earn enough money to stop all together. I just needed the confidence."

We finish our meal but remain at the table, chatting for hours until our conversation is interrupted by the wail of the siren from the town. Something is wrong, I think, and wait to see if my phone rings to summon me. After several minutes it remains silent and I know I'm off the hook. I'm glad, because I'm tired and comfortable and happy at home and I want to stay here. I've had quite a lot of wine to drink and it would be better if I didn't have to drive to a job.

Patricia and I go up the stairs to bed and as I walk past Ollee, I try to get him to go to sleep, but the little dog won't give up on his bone. As I drift off to sleep, I can still hear it grinding against the floor as he gnaws at it. How simple his life is, I think. If only my life was as simple.

Chapter 41

I'm awoken by the sound of the siren wailing. For a moment I think I'm dreaming and in my mind, I'm hearing it from last night. It takes me a minute or two to fully waken. Then I hear my phone ringing and I leap out of bed and answer it. I'm told there's a problem at the café and Roland, the owner, has been taken to hospital with burns to his hands. I immediately think it has something to do with the run-in he had with Edvard, so I tell the operator I'll attend immediately.

By the time I'm dressed and ready to go, Patricia has made me a coffee and buttered me some baguette. She's worried because there seems to be some problem every day now and she's frightened for my safety. I try to reassure her, but in truth, I too am frightened and I'm even beginning to consider putting in for a transfer.

I'm apprehensive as I drive into town, but when I arrive outside the café I'm pleased that, although there's a fire tender present, there's no sign of fire and no smell of smoke. My pleasure is short lived, however, because when I try to enter the building I'm met by my friend Jean who stops me.

"Don't touch anything, Danielle," he says. "Everything is covered in some sort of acid."

I look around the café and I'm shocked. Acid has eaten into the bar and the furniture and even the floor.

"Someone broke in here last night," Jean says. "The owner and his wife were sleeping upstairs and thank goodness, they weren't disturbed. When he came down this morning, this is what he found. He'd touched one of the surfaces and burnt his hands before he realised there was acid on them. He's been taken to hospital for treatment but fortunately, he's not too badly hurt. I've had to call for specialist cleaners from Perpignan. It'll take some time before repairs can be done and the café re-opened. In the meantime, the building must remain closed to everyone, including the owners. This crime was carried out by very ruthless people. The substance they've used can't be bought in the shops and it's highly dangerous to handle. I can't imagine who would do such a thing."

I can think of only one person who has a grudge against Roland and who would be able to source the chemicals, and that person is Edvard Albert. If I was frightened before, I'm terrified now.

I return to the office and once again find myself writing a report to send to Detective Gerard. Surely he can see how bad things have become? Perhaps now he'll offer me some assistance. By the time I've finished writing the report, my colleagues have taken two telephone calls from men who are part of the vigilante group. They're outraged by what's happened to their friend and they're demanding action from the police. Both make threats towards Edvard Albert and, according to them, if we can't deal with him, then they will.

Late in the day Roland arrives at my office to give a statement about what has occurred. His hands are heavily bandaged and I expect him to be shaken and frightened by the incident, but quite the contrary, he is angry and confrontational, and like his friends, he demands action. Once again I find myself offering words of sympathy, but repeating that without evidence, there's nothing I can do.

"Save your sympathy for someone else," he snaps at me, "I don't need it. I just need action and one way or another, I'm going to get it."

I try once again to warn him about taking the law into his own hands, but he just shouts abuse at me, then storms out of my office kicking the wastepaper bin across the room on his way.

My colleague jumps to his feet. "He has no right to speak to you like that," he says and he makes to go after Roland, but I stop him.

"Let him go, he's just letting off steam and he'll calm down soon," I say, but even as the words come out of my mouth, I know I don't believe them.

At the end of the day, I finally receive an email from Detective Gerard but it's just an acknowledgement of the one that I sent to him. He's standing back from this, I think. If I succeed, he'll share in my success, but if I fail, he'll blame me for my shortcomings. He can't lose, but if I mess up, I could lose everything.

Chapter 42

Since the incident at the café, everyone is on edge. The cafe was the main focal point of the town and it was the place where people met on a regular basis. There used to be weekly meetings of groups to play cards or draughts, and the *pétanque* club met there to discuss the league. Without the café, the town feels dead. People no longer congregate in the street to talk, because they would much rather hurry back to the safety of their homes. When they walk past me they no longer greet me, or stop to pass the time of day. Instead, they avert their eyes and walk quickly on. It's as if, in some way, they hold me responsible for their troubles.

Two weeks have passed without any sign of Edvard Albert, but it makes no difference, his presence is still felt here and it overwhelms everyone. If Edvard intended to bring the morale of the town to its knees, then he's succeeded. For the first time ever, local events are being cancelled for fear of not having the attendance. There's a terrible sadness about the place. Our community seems to be falling apart and I don't know what to do about it.

Many people are worried that, with the lack of things to do, local teenagers will become easy pickings for the drug pushers. Parents can't keep their children safely locked up at home for ever, even though many would like to. Since drugs were found at the school, the School Board has cancelled all after hours' activities because they feel the responsibility is too great to ask of the teachers. The final straw came when the annual inter-school dance for senior pupils was cancelled because the other schools, which usually take part, would not allow their pupils to visit our school. Marjorie tried to point out to them that the drug problem is throughout the region. Just because our school is the only one tackling it, it doesn't mean the others are safe, but nothing she said could change their minds.

Patricia tries to cheer me up, but she knows that things are bad. She's changed her mind about giving up her job at the funeral parlour just yet, in case her own business suffers. Fortunately the bulk of her orders for paintings is coming from the gallery in Perpignan and these sales are unaffected by the current problems here. The proprietor is also intending to display some of her work in his other gallery in Narbonne which would increase her exposure.

I awake early on Saturday morning as I'm going to take Patricia to Ceret market, where she's secured a pitch to sell her produce. If she was worried about her business suffering, she had no need. From the moment she arrives, a queue forms and the produce isn't even making it onto her table. I leave her and Ollee and I head for my office as, although it's my day off, I've arranged for Claude's aunt Eveline to come in to see me. I'll go back for Patricia just after twelve, even though the market is open until one o'clock, in case she sells out early and doesn't want to hang around. Claude's Aunt Eveline is waiting at the office when I arrive to open up. I show her to a chair and she's happy to sit down.

"When I was a young woman, I used to run in the mountains," she begins. "Now I can barely walk from the car. I feel so trapped in this useless body and I'm in constant pain. My only relief is from cannabis, so I'm grateful for your understanding. I'm sure it will soon be licensed, because they're doing amazing research in America. It's probably too late for me now because my illness is advancing so quickly, but maybe it will bring relief to others."

I'm very sorry for Eveline, because she's obviously suffering and I feel ashamed that she's thanking me for something I believe should be her right. I assure her, that neither she nor her friends have anything to fear from the police and I wish her well. Then I walk her back to the car where her friend is waiting to drive her home.

I'm barely back through the door when Christian Lesecq arrives, dragging his son Charles along by his collar. He practically throws the boy onto a chair then gives a forceful instruction for him to 'sit' and 'stay' as if he's talking to a pet dog. Then he draws me aside for a private chat.

"He's been selling drugs, Officer," he says. "I caught him red handed, selling drugs from our garage." He takes a package from his pocket and slams it on my desk. "Where would he get the money for this?" he asks. "He won't tell me anything. I've threatened him with everything, from locking him in the house to beating him to a pulp, but he won't answer. I'm hoping you can get some information from him. That's why I've brought him here. Obviously, I don't want my son to have a criminal record but perhaps you could scare him into turning in his supplier. I'm at my wits end with the boy and I need your help."

I sit down at the desk opposite the boy, who is quivering with fear. His face is chalky white and he looks as if he might faint. His t-shirt is ripped with the force of his father dragging him along the street and I feel sorry for the lad. Christian Lesecq is hovering over his son in a very threatening manner. I send him out for a walk, because I don't think the boy will speak while he's in the room.

Once he leaves I say, "Well, Charles you seem to have gotten yourself into rather a mess. Do you want to tell me about it?"

Charles begins to cry and great sobs wrack his skinny frame. "I'm sorry, I'm so sorry," he says. "There was nothing I could do! They were going to hurt my sister if I didn't do what they asked."

"And who exactly are 'they'?"

"I can't say," he answers and fresh tears course down his cheeks. "Don't you understand? They'll hurt my family and they'll kill me, just like they killed Franck Boyer. I don't want to end up in a rubbish bin! If I don't give them the money from selling the drugs they'll cut off my hand just like they did to Franck and if I don't take more drugs to sell they'll hurt my sister."

"If you turn in the person who's threatening you, I'll arrest them and keep them locked up and you'll be safe," I say. "All you need to do is give me a name and it will all be over."

"But it won't, it will never be over because there will always be someone to replace them! I don't deal with the man at the top, and even if I did, you can't get to him, nobody can," he cries, and his body is wracked with sobs once again. His nose is running, but he's too distraught to wipe it.

"Do you know of Edvard Albert?" I ask. "Is he the 'top man' you're speaking about?"

"I can't tell you. I won't tell you anymore, because I don't want to die and I don't want my family to die. Leave me alone!"

He buries his head in his folded arms and I know he'll say nothing more because he's too frightened. When his father returns, I explain to him that his son is under terrible pressure and he's terrified of the people who are supplying him. I also advise him, that whilst I suspect the whole operation is being led by Edvard Albert, everyone is too frightened to turn him in.

"Oh, my poor boy," Christian says. "They've trapped him and now they won't let him go. What can I do to save my son? What can I do to protect my family from these dangerous men?"

I don't have an answer for him because he's in an impossible position. All I can suggest is that he keeps his family close until we can catch the criminals. I'm powerless to do anything until someone is brave enough to give me evidence against Edvard Albert. He has the whole town running scared and I can't see a way out.

I arrive back at the market to collect Patricia, a bit later than I intended. I make my way through the dwindling crowd and I hope she's not been fed up waiting for me. As I approach her table I can see she's sold out of her produce so she's spread the photographs of her paintings on the table for people to see. There are a number of people looking at them and I don't want to disturb her. Ollee is under the table and when the little dog spies me he runs towards me, yipping excitedly. Patricia looks up and I signal to her, 'five minutes', then with Ollee accompanying me I go off to buy her some flowers from the flower seller before the stall holder packs up. When I return, I pack Patricia's table and chair into the car and head for home. As I drive, she counts the money she's earned today onto her lap.

"I've sold everything and I've taken a deposit for my painting of Camprodon," she says happily. "I've decided that I will hand in my notice, because I know I can make this work. I was just nervous because of the way things are in town, but markets are everywhere and I don't have to rely solely on our market. If you don't mind, I'll tell Claude on Monday that I'm giving them notice."

She's had a really good morning and the atmosphere in Ceret market has been exhilarating, but because of this, when we arrive back in our town, we are all the more aware of the changes that have occurred and I feel a heavy cloud of sadness hanging over me once again.

Chapter 43

Sunday is a lazy day for me, but a busy one for Patricia. The stove has four large pans on it bubbling away, this time with apple and blackberry jelly. The apples were given to Patricia by an old gentleman who lives a short distance from our house, on condition that we supply him with an egg from our chickens for his breakfast each day and a jar from each batch of apple jelly for his baguette. He has four apple trees but uses very little of the fruit himself, as it's difficult for him to pick them now because of his age. I've built shelves in our shed so that Patricia can store the apples then use them as and when she needs them. This crop is worth hundreds of euros to her and it's just the boost she needs to give her full-time business a kick start.

I hate leaving the house on Monday morning, as working in town now makes me feel depressed, but I try to stay cheerful for Patricia's sake as I don't want to spoil her day. She's very excited about handing in her notice, because she thought this day would never come. When she telephones me mid-morning, she tells me that Claude offered her a pay rise to stay on, but she's turned it down. Although she has agreed to work two days a month for the higher pay, to help them out until they can find a replacement for her, and I think that's a good compromise.

The day drags on and on and the hands of the clock seem to go slower and slower until at last it is five minutes to six and I prepare to lock up. Inevitably, as I reach the door, the telephone rings and I'm about to ignore it when my mobile rings as well. I answer the office phone and it's the emergency switchboard calling.

"I'm glad I caught you," the voice says, "I was ringing your mobile too, in case you had left the office. A Monsieur Lesecq called and he'd like you to phone him or call on him. He says it's very urgent, something to do with his son. It's not really an emergency, at least I don't think it is, he sounded upset but he wouldn't tell me anything. He just asked for you personally, not for a police response, so it's up to you whether or not you call him back."

I take down his phone number and the address then leave a message for Patricia to say that I'll be late before I head off for the Lesecq residence. When I arrive at the house, the door is opened by Monsieur Lesecq and he's very upset. "It's Charles," he says. "He's missing. He didn't return from school."

I look at my watch and say, "But Monsieur, it is only six-twenty, perhaps he's visiting a friend?"

"No, Officer, you don't understand. I've telephoned all his friends and they've told me he didn't arrive at school today. He's been gone all day. Something's happened to him, because he never misses school, it's the only chance he gets to see his friends these days and besides, they're worried as well."

Now I'm concerned. I don't want to alarm Monsieur Lesecq, but the fate of Franck Boyer is never far from my mind. "Don't worry," I say, "I'll make some calls and we will begin a search for him. I'm sure he's simply run off because he's been frightened by our meeting. Young people always imagine things are worse than they are."

"I'm frightened, Officer, I'm frightened that bastard Edvard Albert has him. The Irishman's son disappeared weeks ago and he never returned."

"That was a very different matter," I reply. "His whole family was involved with drugs and besides, he's an adult, not a schoolboy. I'm sure, that once we begin to search Charles' friend's homes and places of shelter in and around the town, he'll turn up. Try to stay calm."

I'm giving him words of reassurance and I hope my words are true, but I don't really feel confident about what I'm saying. I'm terrified that Edvard, or perhaps one of his men, has grabbed Charles on his way to school. I give Monsieur Lesecq a telephone number to call if he needs to reach me, and I ask him to get in touch if any further information comes to mind, or if Charles returns home. Then I take my leave. Before going home, I return to the office and put the wheels in motion to search for the boy, but with limited resources, I hold out little hope of finding him tonight.

I spend a fitful night and wake in the morning having had very little sleep. When I arrive at the office, I'm told that as well as the police, Monsieur Lesecq and the rest of the vigilante group have been searching for the boy all night, but haven't found him. It's not the news I wanted to hear. I telephone Detective Gerard and explain the situation. This time he does offer assistance by allocating me extra officers to help in the search and letting the police helicopter fly over the mountainside, to see if there is any sign of Charles. If he lit a fire last night to keep warm, or to cook food, the helicopter pilot will spot the smoke.

The news of the missing boy spreads through the area like wildfire, and before very long, dozens of people join in the search for him. By late afternoon I'm beginning to despair because I think another day is going to end with no result. Then I receive a call from a farmer who lives high up in the mountain and he tells me he spotted a boy last night, trying to light a fire beside a tree line. He moved the boy on and told him that if he lit his fire there, he could burn down the whole mountain. The boy answers the description of Charles so I radio the helicopter and give them the location of the farm. I pray that it is Charles, and he's safe, because I couldn't bear the alternative.

My colleague and I remain late at the office, pacing the floor and drinking too much black coffee. At seven-fifteen the phone rings and we both make a grab for it. The boy has been found. He's spent the night on the mountain with no heat or shelter and he's exhausted and very chilled, but otherwise he's well. I'm so relieved that I find myself hugging my colleague and he is hugging me. It's most inappropriate, but at that moment, neither of us cares. I telephone Monsieur Lesecq and inform him his boy is safe and well and he bursts into tears with relief. When he composes himself, I arrange to go around to his house the next day to interview Charles, then I go home for my dinner and most of the contents of a bottle of wine.

Chapter 44

When I arrive at the Lesecq residence to interview Charles, I'm invited in and greeted like a friend. Christian Lesecq is a self-employed businessman and he and his family live in one of the most desirable areas of town. I'm shown into a very plush lounge and invited to sit down on an expensive leather sofa, which probably cost as much as my car. Christian keeps hugging his son and although Charles seems slightly embarrassed, he doesn't stop his father. It's as if Christian has to keep touching the boy to confirm that he's really there. I sit down opposite Charles, and Christian goes off to fetch some coffee.

"Hello Charles," I say. "Are you well?"

The boy bites his bottom lip and nods.

"Do you want to tell me what happened?"

He stares miserably at the floor for a moment or two then he begins to speak. "I had to leave, I had no choice. If I hang around here, they'll hurt my family, but if I'm out of the way they can't blackmail me."

"Will you tell me who 'they' are now?" I ask. "I'd like to help you, if you'll give me the chance."

"I'm sorry, really sorry, but I'll never tell you. I'll run away again, but next time, I'll be better organised so don't bother looking for me."

Christian has returned to the room with the coffees and he's in time to hear what Charles has just said.

"For God's sake, son, haven't you had enough trouble already? Do you think I'd let anything happen to you or this family? You might feel we're powerless against these bastards but I can assure you, we're not. I'm strong and I have strong friends, so don't even consider running away again, because we're all safer if we stick together."

Charles looks helplessly at his father. "Don't you see, Dad, these men are murderers and they don't stick to any rules. What chance would someone like you or me have against the likes of them?"

"The boy is correct, Monsieur Lesecq," I say. "These are very dangerous men and you must not try to take the law into your own hands, or your family might be at even more risk."

"I hear what you're saying, Officer," he replies. "But it's clear to me your hands are tied because everyone is too frightened to talk. I must warn you that I will protect my family at any cost."

We sit in silence for a moment, as each of us considers what the other has said. I have one more attempt at getting Charles to talk to me, but it's no use as he is flatly refusing to say any more. Christian has stopped pressing his son to speak to me and I'm afraid, that after I leave, he'll get the answers I so badly require and use those answers himself.

I leave the house with a heavy heart because I can't help this family. I'm frightened that Monsieur Lesecq will approach Edvard to try to warn him off and end up suffering the consequences of such a foolhardy act. I understand the anger he feels and his desire to protect his family, but if it were my family that was at such risk, I wouldn't try to deal with it myself. More likely I'd pack up and move away. It's far better to be a coward and run, than to be a dead hero. I drive back to the town centre and stop at the bar where I see Byron sitting at a table outside.

"Hello, dear lady," he says when I approach. "Will you join me?"

I am reluctant to return to the office so I sit down on a chair beside him. Byron is always a good listener and I value his advice. I find myself telling him about Charles running off, Christian Lesecq's response, and what he said to me about the strength of him and his friends.

"You said it yourself, Danielle, your hands are tied. If this vigilante group choose to break the law, then that's up to them. If you're lucky, the problem will go away, and if not, you can arrest these people, as and when they break the law. In the meantime, if I were in your shoes, I wouldn't fret about what may or may not happen. You can't take responsibility for the mistakes of others and if you allow yourself to succumb to that kind of pressure, you'll give yourself a stroke. Let it go, Danielle, just let it go."

He pauses, raises his eyebrows, and smiles and nods at me. I find myself smiling and nodding back. Then he asks Brigitte to bring us a *demi de rouge* and two glasses, and as we drink the rich red wine, I begin to relax. I feel better for receiving good advice from my friend. I can always rely on Byron.

Chapter 45

Over the next few days I see Christian, Roland and the other vigilantes congregating at the bar. There are still five of them, because although a new face has joined them, one of the others has dropped out of the group. If I pass them by, they immediately stop talking and it worries me. I'm sure they're plotting something and it's driving me crazy because I don't know what it is.

The work on the café is progressing quite quickly and I hope it will reopen soon and things can get back to normal. Roland seems to be the leader of the vigilante group. While his café is out of commission, he has too much time on his hands and it's not healthy.

Charles Lesecq is delivered to school in the morning then collected after school every day, by his father or one of his father's friends, and I've never seen him out alone. It's obvious that Christian is protecting his son and at the same time, ensuring that he doesn't take off again.

The school is searched regularly for drugs and the School Board now employs a security guard to check that pupils arrive and leave at the correct time. If a pupil doesn't turn up for school, the parents are immediately informed. Truancy will not be tolerated because if they are not in school and they are not at home, then they're at risk. The children are young adults and are outraged by the restrictions imposed upon them, but as they're still minors, it's their parents who are in charge and they're delighted.

A few weeks go by without incident. The café reopens for business and it's a relief. It's as if the heart of the town is beating again and gradually the various groups begin to meet there. The people of our town are starting to relax and friends are beginning to stop and talk to each other in the street once more. I'm hopeful that our troubles are now over and things will return to normal, but when I say this to Byron, he's cautious. He tells me to wait and see, and unfortunately, as usual, he's right.

It's the first day of October and it's a bright and sunny morning. I'm walking to the café for my mid-morning coffee when I see Eddy's car parked across the road. My heart sinks. It stands out like a sore thumb because, apart from Roland's white van, it's the only vehicle in the street. When I enter the café, Roland and his friends are sitting at a table inside. They are deep in conversation, so I'm served by Roland's wife. She seems agitated and she keeps looking out of the window at the car.

Apart from the vigilantes, I'm the only person in the café and I feel awkward sitting here alone while they stare at me, silently willing me to leave. I finish my coffee quickly and head back to the office. As I pass the Mercedes, I see that Eddy is leaning against it and he nods an acknowledgement to me which I ignore. The street has suddenly emptied of people and even Eddy's driver is nowhere to be seen. I make my way along the street towards the office without looking back. A huge weight of disappointment rests on my shoulders, because I'd hoped we'd seen the last of Edvard Albert.

When I return to the office, I telephone Patricia to see what she's up to. I need to hear her sweet voice and share in her happiness. Now that she's running her own business, she's always full of good news and her enthusiasm is infectious. She tells me she's baking apple pies for a restaurant in St. Jean, and apple cakes for a shop in Ceret, and Ollee chased a rabbit today and nearly caught it, and the lady who lives in the house on the road into town gave her a bag of pears in exchange for some eggs. All this information in one excited sentence gives my spirits a lift and I can't wait for the day to be over, so I can go home and be with her.

Apart from when I go out to drive some files over to Ceret, I remain in the office and clock watch. Finally, my working day does draw to an end and I drive to the café to buy a bottle of wine to take home. I see that Eddy's car is still parked across the road. It's been parked there for hours and he doesn't usually hang around for long. There's no sign of Eddy or his driver. Out of sight, out of mind, I think, and I hum to myself as I drive home to my sanctuary.

Chapter 46

In the morning I leave a bit earlier than usual for work, as I've arranged to make a couple of deliveries for Patricia. Consequently, I take a slightly different route. I'm driving down the main street towards the café when I see that Eddy's car is still parked in exactly the same place as it was yesterday. It's still parked illegally, with the front half of the car covering a cross hatched area reserved for the disabled. As I slowly drive past, I notice that it's sustained some damage to its side, so I pull in to take a closer look.

When I examine the car I see the wing mirror has been struck and it's smashed to pieces. There are deep scratches the length of the body and a slight dent in the door. All the damage looks as if it's been caused by another vehicle swerving into it. I'm surprised when I look inside the car to see the key is still in the ignition, and when I try the door, it's open. How strange, I think. I wonder where the driver is.

I look about the street, but it's practically empty at this time of the morning. There are one or two people out and about, collecting their baguettes for breakfast from the *boulangerie*, which is further along the street, but apart from them, the street is quiet. I take the key from the ignition and use it to lock up, then I go to the café to see if Roland can tell me anything.

When I enter, I see Monsieur Lesecq standing at the bar talking to Roland. They're laughing and joking with one another. This time they don't stop chatting when I approach.

"Bonjour, Officer. Bonjour, *ca va*?" Lesecq says.

"It's another beautiful morning, how are you today?" Roland adds.

"*Tres bien, merci*," I reply. "I've come to ask you about the car parked across the street. It seems to have sustained some damage, and when I looked inside, I found that the keys were in the ignition. Do you know anything about the car? Have you seen anybody near it?"

"It's been parked there since yesterday," Lesecq replies.

"It belongs to Edvard Albert, but you probably know that already," Roland adds. "It's bad for my business having it stopped right across the street, because people won't come in if they think Eddy is around. You've no doubt noticed that it's illegally parked. It's in a tow-away zone, so I'd be obliged if you'd arrange to have it towed. My business has suffered enough at that man's hands already."

The two men glance nervously at one another, as if unsure whether or not they've overstepped the mark with their request.

I look at them both for a minute, then I smile slowly and reply. "You are quite correct, Messieurs. Of course it must be towed. I'll arrange for it to be done, as soon as I return to my office."

They exhale their bated breath and a look of relief crosses their faces. Once again, they grin at each other and then at me. Without being asked, Roland pours me a coffee and places it on the bar beside Christian's cup. "You'll join us for a cup of coffee, won't you, Danielle?" he asks.

"Yes Roland, *merci*," I reply and the subtle distinction of being addressed by my first name, instead of my position, is not lost on me.

When I get back to the office, I arrange to have the car impounded and then I telephone Magda Gold, to see if she has any idea why it's been left unattended. I can tell by her voice she's reluctant to talk to me, but after some persuasion, she tells me that both Eddy and his driver should have called at her house yesterday, but they didn't turn up. When pressed, she does give me the name of Eddy's driver and she tells me he lives somewhere in Barcelona, but she doesn't know where. Neither, it seems, does she have an address for Eddy. I'm content there's nothing more I can do – or indeed, want to do – so as far as I'm concerned, the matter is closed.

Chapter 47

It's been several days since I had Eddy's car towed away and nobody has come forward to claim it. I'm surprised that the driver left the keys in the ignition and didn't return, but the truth is, I really don't care. If the car isn't claimed, after a time it will be sold and that will be the end of it.

Eddy hasn't been seen in town – the only person looking for him is Magda Gold and she's reported him missing. She's come into my office a couple of times now, to ask if he's been seen. I'm delighted when she tells me, that on the day he seems to have vanished, he'd made an appointment to meet her to pay her some money she was owed. She wouldn't tell me exactly how much, but for her to be so anxious to discover his whereabouts, it must be a sizeable sum. She says she's been unable to trace Eddy or his driver in France or in Spain. She's worried that they might have come to harm as it was very odd for the car to be abandoned with the keys inside. I assure her I'll do everything in my power to find them, but I think she knows I'm lying. I don't care. I'm delighted they're gone.

With the change of season my work load has lessened and I prefer it that way. I have more time to spend helping Patricia with her business and my colleagues and I can take the occasional extra day off and nobody is any the wiser.

I now take my mid-morning coffee in the café where I'm never charged, and once more I'm greeted by people wherever I go and I'm pleased to be popular again. No one has actually voiced an opinion yet, but everyone is hoping that the changing season has heralded a change throughout the town, a change away from drugs and gangsters. A change for the better.

I'm sitting inside the café drinking my coffee because a brief autumnal rain shower has soaked all the tables and chairs outside, when my mobile begins to ring. When I look at the number I see it's the emergency operator calling, so I take the call. A woman's voice reports to me.

"A body has been found in the river, approximately one kilometre from the south bridge. Can you attend?"

I confirm I'll go immediately and ask her to contact the other services for me. She tells me Dr. Poullet is on call and he will also attend. My old friend, I think, here we go again. I'm driving slowly along the road, much to the annoyance of the other drivers who are stuck behind me, because I'm trying to find where I'm meant to go and the instructions and directions I've been given are not very helpful. Eventually, I spot a fire tender pulled onto a grass verge and I realise I've reached my destination, so I park the car and head down a narrow track on foot. I arrive at the scene just as the body is being hauled from the river. One of the *pompiers* is in the river, guiding the body onto the bank and it's being hauled up by a rope, unceremoniously secured around its ankles. I hear huffing and puffing behind me and I turn to see Dr. Poullet coming my way. He's slipping and sliding along the steep track and grumbling to himself as he struggles along.

"Why do all emergencies these days turn out to be corpses? Can you not find me a baby to deliver, or better still, a simple fall or a bee sting? Why do I have to clamber over rocks or down muddy tracks? Does nobody die in the street or at home any more? Bonjour, Danielle," he nods at me. "Bonjour, Jean," he nods at the chief *pompier*. "Well, let us see, who have we here?" he adds looking in the direction of the corpse.

The body is dragged fully onto the bank then rolled over onto its back. Even in its battered and bloated condition, I recognise immediately that it's the body of Edvard Albert.

"The river has done significant damage," Dr. Poullet says. He dons thin rubber gloves and then turns the head first one way, then the other. "There is substantial damage to the skull and the whole body has been broken on the rocks as it travelled downstream. Where exactly was it found?"

Jean steps forward and explains that a fisherman saw the corpse snagged on a tree branch as he went to cast his line. "It's the biggest thing he's ever likely to catch," he adds, laughing.

It always amazes me that we can find humour where others would find horror.

"I wouldn't be surprised if he's fallen into the river, struck his head then drowned," Dr. Poullet comments. "I'll know better once we cut him open. I'd be willing to bet that we find river water in his lungs. I had a similar case some years ago, when a young man went for a walk with friends along the riverbank and fell in. He couldn't be rescued, because the speed of the river had battered him senseless against the rocks and carried him away."

Dr. Poullet gives me a knowing look, and in that instant, I realise that he too recognises this corpse. He's testing me, to see if I'm likely to agree with this explanation of how Edvard met his death. He would like to find this to be an accidental death, because anything else could open up a can of worms and nobody wants that.

"I'm sure you'll be correct, Doctor," I reply. "If you find water in the lungs, then of course, it's most likely to be an unfortunate accident. He stares hard into my eyes for a moment and I stare back and nod and we both know we've reached an understanding. As far as I'm concerned, this gangster has met a timely end and the sooner we can wrap up this case, the sooner we'll be rid of him once and for all.

I search the pockets of Edvard's jacket, in case Magda's money is still on the body, but I find no sign of it. Although surprisingly, even after his battering in the river, his wallet containing a few euros and credit cards is still in his pocket and this adds strength to the probability of accidental death, because if foul play occurred, surely his wallet would be missing.

"Let us hope I'm correct," Dr. Poullet says and I nod in agreement.

I take my leave of the scene and return to the office to write up my report. Doctor Poullet has promised me that I'll have his written findings within forty-eight hours and he says he'll telephone me as soon as he looks at the lungs.

I'm ecstatically happy now the body's been found, because with Edvard gone, all my worries and fears will be over. I can't help smiling at the thought of sending my report to Detective Gerard. Things just keep getting better and better.

Chapter 48

Within a very short time the word is out about Edvard's death. The phone at the office is ringing off the hook with people calling to confirm the news. The impact that his death has caused is huge, and dozens of people have called in to the office to congratulate me and my colleagues. Many have brought gifts of chocolates or wine, and we're overwhelmed. My colleagues and I take the joint decision to lock up and go home early, and we divide the gifts as equally as we can. When I arrive home, even Patricia, who has been at the house all day, knows the news.

"Marjorie phoned," she explains. "I've taken loads of orders today and I think it's because everyone is so much happier. What better way to celebrate than with Patricia's pies?" she says with a grin.

"How about with two litres of wine and a ton of chocolates?" I ask, and I show her my loot.

"It really is fantastic news, Danielle. Do you want to go out to dinner to celebrate?"

I explain about all the people telephoning and calling at the office, and because of this, we decide to stay at home so we can have a quiet dinner together. We drink a bucket load of wine and eat chocolates until we feel sick. When we go to bed I fall asleep as soon as my head hits the pillow.

As I travel into work the next morning, the sky seems bluer, the sun brighter and the colours of the trees on the mountains deeper – everything is richer. It's as if the dark shadow that's been hanging over our town has lifted and I can see clearly once more.

Of all the phone calls received today, only three are passed to me by my colleagues. They're trying to save me from my success and I'm grateful to them, because even heroes need time to gather their thoughts and the telephone is ringing incessantly.

The first call that I take is from Magda Gold. She wants to know if I found her money on Eddy's body and when I tell her I didn't, she's enraged. She tells me she hates this town and everyone in it and she says we're all thieves. I listen to her rant then as calmly as I can, I suggest that perhaps she should consider moving, after all, there's really nothing left here for her now.

The second call is from Siobhan O'Brien and she can hardly speak with weeping. She tells me her son Collum has returned home – 'back from the dead', are her exact words. She then informs me that Aidan has a buyer for the farm and they plan to move north before the winter. They intend to run a small guest house in Marseilles, because they feel their children need to be part of a busier community. Out of the frying pan, into the fire, I think. They really are very stupid people. If Collum could get involved with drugs in this town, just think what he could get up to in a lawless place like Marseilles. The third call comes in late in the day, and it's from Dr. Poullet.

"Just as I thought," he says, "lungs are full of water and evidence of a bang to the head, several actually. Accidental death from drowning is the cause of death and I'll write that on the death certificate if you're satisfied with my findings."

"I'm content with that, Dr. Poullet," I reply. "We can close the book on this case now and ship the body home."

"And where exactly is his home?" the doctor asks. "Do we know?"

174

"I've been given an address for him in Barcelona. So I'm sending the body to Spain. Let them deal with it. I'll be glad to be rid of him."

"If only we could send all our problems to Spain," he sighs. "I have a couple of really annoying patients who I'd love to send over the border."

I chat to Doctor Poullet for a few minutes because I find him very amusing and besides, we have an understanding now. There are unsaid words that bind us together and I want to wallow in our camaraderie for a few moments before I return to my other work. After we do say our goodbyes, I sit at my desk and check my mail on the computer. There is an email from Detective Gerard which I open. It simply says 'Well done, problem solved'. While I'm happy with his praise, I have to say that I expected more, much more. I feel the very least I deserve is a phone call and I was hoping for a visit. Not just an ordinary visit, but one with waving flags, banging drums and ticker tape. It seems the more successful I become, the less contact I have with him, but maybe that's how it should be. Perhaps I'm being naïve to expect anything else.

Chapter 49

The days roll into weeks and everything returns to normal. It's as if we stepped out of kilter for a while and now the world has turned and all is well again. Patricia has become self-employed full-time and the change has been almost seamless. It feels as if she's always sold her pickles, pies and paintings. She's designed her own brand now and all her produce is labelled and marketed under her name. Shops and restaurants telephone with their orders, which she writes down in her book at the kitchen table. I'm sure many of them think they're telephoning some fancy establishment and not the kitchen of our little house. Her produce is always in demand, and if we were worried about her not earning enough, we needn't have been. Her paintings are also selling well and with galleries displaying her work in both Perpignan and Narbonne, she's earning more than me.

Patricia has rescued three more chickens and we have been adopted by a slim, beautiful, ginger and white cat that we've named Mimi. Ollee wasn't too sure of her at first, but she's won him over. He now tolerates her drinking water from his bowl and sleeping on his blanket, when the mood takes her.

Patricia and I are sitting at the table chatting about how good our lives have become. She's speaking about the black weeks when Edvard Albert blighted out town and I have the urge to tell her the truth about him and the day when he vanished. I've kept the details to myself until now, but I feel this is the right moment in time for confession and confession is good for the soul, so they say.

I begin by telling Patricia that on the first day of October I went to the café for my mid-morning coffee and saw Eddy leaning against his car, which was parked across the road. I tell her I was very disappointed, because I'd hoped he wouldn't return to our town. When I entered the café I saw that the vigilantes were holding a meeting and they were deep in conversation. Lesecq's white van was parked outside the café, diagonally opposite Eddy's car. I felt uncomfortable standing in the café, being the only customer, so I returned to the office because I had some files to deliver to Ceret.

I immediately picked up my car and left to deliver the files, but because I was parked facing the opposite direction to where I was heading, I drove along the road until I reached a side street where I could turn and drive back. I'd just turned out of the side street when I realised that I hadn't shut the boot properly, so I pulled in and got out of the car to secure it.

It was at that moment I heard a bang and I looked up to see Lesecq's white van being driven down the road. He had done a u-turn at speed, misjudged the room he had, and hit Eddy's car. As I watched, the back door of the van flew open and I could see inside. I saw Eddy being held by two of the vigilantes as the van slowed down for a third man to secure the door. For a moment, I didn't know what to do, but then I jumped back into my car and followed them, at a discreet distance.

Patricia stands and pours us both coffees then she places a cup in front of me on the table before she sits back down. She gently pats my arm and asks me to continue and I do.

I tell her that I followed them for about a kilometre before they pulled off the road and set off down a track towards the river. I parked my car a short distance behind so they wouldn't see it when they left, then I quickly walked down the track to look for them. At the end of the track is a small clearing and that's where they were.

I observed as each of the men in turn shouted at Eddy. They were warning him to leave town and they were threatening him. He was laughing at them, but I could see he was scared. Then Eddy said something that I couldn't hear and Roland went crazy and started punching him and the others joined in. They were using him like a punch bag. After a few moments, Eddy dropped to the ground, groaning. I saw an envelope fall out of his pocket and Roland picked it up. I thought he'd stuffed it back into the pocket, but I couldn't be sure. Then Roland delivered a kick to Eddy's head, which rendered him unconscious. The group stood talking for a minute or two before leaving, abandoning Eddy where he lay.

They walked right past me as I hid in the bushes, but they didn't see me. After a few moments I left my hiding place and walked back up the track to check that they were gone. As I looked along the road, I saw Lesecq's white van in the distance.

Patricia sips her coffee and I pause to sip some of mine, considering what to say next.

"Did they kill him?" Patricia asks. Her eyes are wide and she's staring at me.

"Not exactly," I reply. "When I walked back down the track I arrived at the clearing just in time to see Eddy drag himself to the river's edge. He was disorientated and in his semi- conscious state, he couldn't judge where he was and he slipped into the water."

"Oh my God," Patricia says, and she clasps her hand over her mouth.

I hold my head in my hands and say, "I couldn't save him Patricia. The river was fast flowing and deep at that spot and his body was carried away before I could reach him."

I look up through my partially-open fingers to see how she is receiving this news.

Finally, she speaks. "There was absolutely nothing you could have done, Danielle. You could have drowned if you'd entered the water, and besides, if anyone deserved to die it was Eddy. He's blighted so many lives and I'm sure that he's been responsible for more than one death."

It was the response I was hoping for, because I too, felt he deserved to die.

"You were right to say nothing," she continues. "After all, he was alive when the vigilante group left him and arresting them would have made no difference. You must have felt awful at not being able to save him. I'm so sorry you had to witness something so terrible. I do have one question though, Danielle. Where was his driver, when Eddy was taken from the street?"

"I have no idea, but he wasn't in sight, so perhaps he'd been sent on an errand. I did see him standing at the car later in the day, then he disappeared. Maybe that was why the keys were left in the ignition. Maybe he left them for Eddy when he took off."

"Please try and put the whole business from your mind," she says. "It's over now, my darling."

Patricia stands and places a protective arm around my shoulders and she gives me a hug. Actually, I didn't feel awful about not saving Eddy. In fact, I felt very happy when I watched him being battered against the rocks as the river carried him away, because he deserved his fate. Now that I've told Patricia about his death, I feel light and unburdened. I suggest we take Ollee for a stroll in the garden to get some air.

We're looking at our flowering plants when I notice that one of them has grass growing around it, strangling the roots. With no hesitation, I pluck out the grass and the flower bed is perfect once again. There's no room for grass in my flower bed, or for that matter, in my town.

Chapter 50

ANOTHER TRUTH

To think that one small act could change so much is amazing. On the first day of October, I entered the café to have my mid-morning coffee and I could see the vigilante group were sitting around a table having a meeting. They were deep in conversation and were unaware that I overheard what they were discussing.

I heard them planning to grab Eddy off the street one day and drive him to the clearing by the river, then frighten him into leaving town. I don't suppose they expected the opportunity to arise so quickly. I could have stepped in and stopped them there and then, but I chose not to.

I witnessed him being taken that day and I knew exactly where the group were going. That's why I could travel so far behind Lesecq's van and not be seen. I watched them take Eddy from the van and drag him to the clearing where they beat him. Then I watched them leave him, semi-conscious on the ground, before getting back into the van and driving off.

Once they'd gone I went over to Eddy and he was drifting in and out of consciousness. At one point, he focussed on my face and spoke to me. "Help me, Officer," he said, "It's your duty to help me. I want to press charges against those men. I know you saw what happened. I saw you watching them when they were beating me. I saw you."

He tried to get up and he was in a kneeling position when I kicked him on the head. I couldn't have him tell anyone that I'd witnessed what happened to him and ignored it, and I didn't want to make criminals out of good men. When he fell back to the ground I kicked him again, to make sure he wouldn't get up.

It was hard work dragging his unconscious body to the riverside, but quite easy to roll him into the river. My only regret was not checking his pockets first, as I later discovered he was carrying a lot of money, but then again, maybe Roland had taken it already.

When I saw him being battered against the rocks I knew he would die, particularly as I saw his head strike one of the rocks. It was just a question of whether the impact finished him off, or the drowning. If his body hadn't been snagged under a tree, he would probably have been discovered later that day and I was a bit concerned when he didn't turn up.

Still, all's well that ends well.

# # #

A Message from Danielle

Thank you for reading 'Grass Grows in the Pyrenees. I do hope you enjoyed it.

Perhaps you think you know me very well, but life is full of changes and Palm Trees in The Pyrenees was the start of my journey. If you would like to know more about me, and the place where I live, then you now have further opportunity.

Also written by Elly Grant in this series are 'Red Light in the Pyrenees', 'Dead End in the Pyrenees' and 'Deadly degrees in the Pyrenees. Also, if you haven't already seen it, you may like 'Palm Trees in the Pyrenees.' You may also like to read Elly's other books.

Till soon
Danielle

Acknowledgement

For my husband for believing in me, Pamela Duncan for her continued support.

Other books by Elly Grant

Palm Trees in the Pyrenees
Take one rookie female cop
Add a dash or two of mysterious death
And a heap of prejudice and suspicion
Place all in a small French spa town
And stir well
Turn up the heat
And simmer until thoroughly cooked
The result will be surprising

Grass Grows in the Pyrenees gives an insight into the workings and atmosphere of a small French town and the surrounding mountains, in the Eastern Pyrenees. The story unfolds told by Danielle, a single, thirty-year-old, cop. The sudden and mysterious death of a local farmer suspected of growing cannabis opens a 'Pandora's' box of trouble. It's a race against time to stop the gangsters before the town, and everyone in it, is damaged beyond repair.

sample - Chapter 1

His death occurred quickly and almost silently. It took only seconds of tumbling and clawing at air before the inevitable thud as he hit the ground. He landed in the space in front of the bedroom window of the basement apartment. As no-one was home at the time and, as the flat was actually below ground level, he may have gone unnoticed but for the insistent yapping of the scrawny, aged poodle belonging to the equally scrawny and aged Madame Laurent.

Indeed, everything in the town continued as normal for a few moments. The husbands who'd been sent to collect the baguettes for breakfast had stopped, as usual, at the bar to enjoy a customary glass of pastis and a chat with the patron and other customers. Women gathered in the little square beside the river, where the daily produce market took place, to haggle for fruit, vegetables and honey before moving the queue to the boucherie to choose the meat for their evening meals.

Yes, that day began like any other. It was a cold, crisp, February morning and the sky was a bright, clear blue just as it had been every morning since the start of the year. The yellow Mimosa shone out luminously in the morning sunshine from the dark green of the Pyrenees.

Gradually, word filtered out of the boucherie and down the line of waiting women that the first spring lamb of the season had made its way onto the butcher's counter and everyone wanted some. Conversation switched from whether Madame Portes actually grew the Brussels sprouts she sold on her stall, or simply bought them at the supermarket in Perpignan then resold them at a higher price, to speculating whether or not there would be sufficient lamb to go round. A notable panic rippled down the queue at the very thought of there not being enough as none of the women wanted to disappoint her family. That would be unacceptable in this small Pyrenean spa town, as in this small town, like many others in the region a woman's place as housewife and mother was esteemed and revered. Even though many held jobs outside the home, their responsibility to their family was paramount.

Yes, everyone followed their usual routine until the siren blared out – twice. The siren was a wartime relic that had never been decommissioned even though the war had ended over half a century before. It was retained as a means of summoning the pompiers, who were not only the local firemen but also paramedics. One blast of the siren was used when there was a minor road accident or if someone took unwell at the spa but two blasts was for something extremely serious.

The last time there were two blasts was when a very drunken Jean-Claude accidentally shot Monsieur Reynard while mistaking him for a boar. Fortunately Monsieur Reynard recovered, but he still had a piece of shot lodged in his head which caused his eye to squint when he was tired. This served as a constant reminder to Jean-Claude of what he'd done as he had to see Monsieur Reynard every day in the cherry orchard where they both worked.

On hearing two blasts of the siren everyone stopped in their tracks and everything seemed to stand still. A hush fell over the town as people strained to listen for the shrill sounds of the approaching emergency vehicles. Some craned their necks skyward hoping to see the police helicopter arrive from Perpignan and, whilst all were shocked that something serious had occurred, they were also thrilled by the prospect of exciting, breaking news. Gradually, the chattering restarted. Shopping was forgotten and the market abandoned. The boucherie was left unattended as its patron followed the crowd of women making their way to the main street. In the bar the glasses of pastis were hastily swallowed instead of being leisurely sipped as everyone rushed to see what had happened.

As well as police and pompiers, a large and rather confused group of onlookers arrived outside an apartment building owned by an English couple called Carter. They arrived on foot and on bicycles. They brought ageing relatives, pre-school children, prams and shopping. Some even brought their dogs. Everyone peered and stared and chatted to each other. It was like a party without the balloons or streamers.

There was a buzz of nervous excitement as the police from the neighbouring larger town began to cordon off the area around the apartment block with tape. Monsieur Brune was told in no uncertain terms to restrain his dog, as it kept running over to where the body lay, and was contaminating the area in more ways than one.

A slim woman wearing a crumpled linen dress was sitting on a chair in the paved garden of the apartment block, just inside the police line. Her elbows rested on her knees and she held her head in her hands. Her limp, brown hair hung over her face. Every so often she lifted her chin, opened her eyes and took in great, gasping breaths of air as if she was in danger of suffocating. Her whole body shook. Madame Carter, Belinda, hadn't actually fainted but she was close to it. Her skin was clammy and her pallor grey. Her eyes threatened at any moment to roll back in their sockets and blot out the horror of what she'd just seen.

She was being supported by her husband, David, who was visibly shocked. His tall frame sagged as if his thin legs could no longer support his weight and he kept swiping away tears from his face with the backs of his hands. He looked dazed and, from time to time, he covered his mouth with his hand as if trying to hold in his emotions but he was completely overcome.

The noise from the crowd became louder and more excitable and words like accident, suicide and even murder abounded. Claudette, the owner of the bar that stood across the street from the incident, supplied the chair on which Belinda now sat. She realized that she was in a very privileged position, being inside the police line, so Claudette stayed close to the chair and Belinda. She patted the back of Belinda's hand distractedly, while endeavouring to overhear tasty morsels of conversation to pass on to her rapt audience. The day was turning into a circus and everyone wanted to be part of the show.

Finally, a specialist team arrived. There were detectives, uniformed officers, secretaries, people who dealt with forensics and even a dog handler. The tiny police office was not big enough to hold them all so they commandeered a room at the Mairie, which is our town hall.

It took the detectives three days to take statements and talk to the people who were present in the building when the man, named Steven Gold, fell. Three days of eating in local restaurants and drinking in the bars much to the delight of the proprietors. I presumed these privileged few had expense accounts, a facility we local police did not enjoy. I assumed that my hard earned taxes paid for these expense accounts yet none of my so called colleagues asked me to join them.

They were constantly being accosted by members of the public and pumped for information. Indeed everyone in the town wanted to be their friend and be a party to a secret they could pass on to someone else. There was a buzz of excitement about the place that I hadn't experienced for a very long time. People who hadn't attended church for years suddenly wanted to speak to the priest. The doctor who'd attended the corpse had a full appointment book. And everyone wanted to buy me a drink so they could ask me questions. I thought it would never end. But it did. As quickly as it had started, everybody packed up, and then they were gone.

Red Light in the Pyrenees
Take one respected female cop
Add two or three drops of violent death
Some ladies of the night
And a bucket full of blood
Place all in, and around, a small French spa town
Stir constantly with money and greed
Until all becomes clear
The result will be very satisfying

Red Light in the Pyrenees, third in the series Death in the Pyrenees, gives you an insight into the workings and atmosphere of a small French town in the Eastern Pyrenees. The story unfolds, told by Danielle, a single, thirty-something, female cop. The sudden and violent death of a local Madam brings fear to her working girls and unsettles the town. But doesn't every cloud have a silver lining? Danielle follows the twists and turns of events until a surprising truth is revealed. Hold your breath, it's a bumpy ride.

sample - Chapter 1

The body of Madame Henriette is lying through the broken window of the kitchen door with the lower part of the frame supporting her lifeless corpse. Her head, shoulder and one arm hang outside, while the rest of her remains inside, as if she has endeavoured to fly, Superman style, through the window and become stuck. She is slumped, slightly bent at the knees, but with both feet still touching the floor. Her body is surrounded by jagged shards of broken glass.

From the kitchen this is all one sees. It is not until you open the window to the side of the door and look through it that you see the blood. Indeed quite a large area of the tiny courtyard has been spattered with gore as Madame Henriette's life has pumped out of her. One shard has sliced through her throat and, by the amount of blood around, it seems to have severed her jugular. She must have been rendered unconscious almost immediately as she has made no effort to lift herself off the dagger-like pieces of glass which are sticking out from the frame.

There is blood on the pot plants and on the flowering creeper which grows up the wall, dividing this house from the neighbour's. It has also sprayed the small, hand crafted, wrought iron table and chairs. The blood is beginning to turn black in the morning sun and there's a sizeable puddle congealing on the ground under the body. This will need to be spread with sawdust when the clean up begins, I think to myself.

There is rather a lot of blood on Madame Henriette's head as it has run down her face from the gaping wound on her throat, but it's still possible to see that her hair is well-styled and her face is fully made up. Her clothes are tight and rather too sexy for a woman of her age and her push-up bra and fish-net stockings seem inappropriate at this time of the morning. If you didn't know any better, you would assume that Madame Henriette is simply a lady of growing years trying desperately to hold on to her youth, but to her neighbours and those of us who have had dealings with her, the truth is much less forgiving. Madame Henriette is indeed a Madame. She is a lady of the night, a peddler of prostitutes, and this building which she owns is a brothel.

The house of Madame Henriette is situated in the old part of town where the cobbled streets are so narrow that only one car may pass at a time. All the buildings are tall and slim and made of stone. Each is distinguished from the next by different coloured shutters and different degrees of weathering to the facade.

When entering this house, one would pass through a small door which is cut in a much larger, heavier one. The magnificent carved entrance looks overdressed in this street and harks back to a time when this area was much grander. Nowadays everyone wants modern and the town has spread out with alarming speed from this central point. The wealthy live in the suburbs. They have gardens, swimming pools and pizza ovens. From once being uptown and chic, these streets have become dreary and they now contain a lower class of citizen. They are a melting pot of students, foreigners and people who survive on state benefits. Sometimes holidaymakers rent here thinking the area is quaint and having the desire to experience a 'typical' French house in a 'typical' French street.

After entering through the door, which is immediately off the road, you would find yourself in a narrow hallway with a magnificent, old and ornate, tiled floor. A curved stone stairway with an iron banister rail then takes you to the upper floors. On the first floor, if you turned to your right, you would find yourself in the sitting room where Madame Henriette offered her guests some wine as they waited for one of her 'nieces' to fetch them. Then they would be taken to one of the bedrooms which are situated on the upper floors. To the left is the kitchen but few meals were cooked there. Food was usually very quickly thrown together from a selection of cold meats, cheese and bread, then hastily eaten by the girls as they grabbed a few spare moments between clients. All, of course, was washed down with glasses of heavy, red, cheap, local wine. The wine made both the food and the clients more palatable.

The body of Madame Henriette was discovered by her maid Eva who is a rather scrawny girl aged about twenty. She has mousy brown hair and grubby looking skin peppered with acne scars. Every day Eva came to work for Madame, her duties being to wash the sheets, clean the house and bring in the food from the market. She was also responsible for buying condoms and checking that each bedroom had a plentiful supply. Madame Henriette was fastidious about health and safety and would never allow sexual contact without condoms.

On discovering the body of her mistress, the shocked young woman fled the house and ran screaming into the street. One of the neighbours heard the screams and chose, on this occasion, not to ignore the noises coming from the vicinity of the house but instead telephoned for the emergency services and this is where my story begins.

Dead End in the Pyrenees
Take a highly respected female cop
Add a bunch of greedy people
And place all in a small French town
Throw in a large helping of opportunity, lies and deceit
Add a pinch in prejudice
A twist of resentment

And dot with death and despair.
Be prepared for some shocking revelations
Dangerous predators are everywhere
Then sit down, relax and enjoy
With a dash or two of humour
And plenty of curiosity

Dead End in the Pyrenees is the fourth book in Elly Grant's Death in the Pyrenees series. Follow Danielle, a female cop located in a small town on the French side of the Pyrenees as she tries to solve a murder at the local spa. This story is about life in a small French town, local events, colourful characters, prejudice and of course death.

sample – Chapter 1

The blow to his head wasn't hard enough to render Monsieur Dupont unconscious but it stupefied him. Blood poured profusely from a deep scalp wound down into his left eye. He flopped onto the recently washed tiles at the side of the Roman bath then floundered at the edge, frantically trying to stop his body from slipping completely into the pool. His upper torso overhung the edge, his hands slapping at the water as he tried to right himself. He was aware of the metal chair, which was attached to a hoist to enable the disabled to enter the water, beginning to descend. As it lowered, it trapped Monsieur Dupont, forcing his head and shoulders under the water. He struggled, his toes drumming the moist tiles, his arms making a flapping motion, but he was hopelessly stuck. Soon he succumbed. Brimstone smelling steam rose from the surface of the spa pool and silence returned.

When Madame Georges arrived for work, she was surprised to hear a low, electronic, whirring sound coming from the pool area. She couldn't think what it was. Surely the machinery and gadgets, designed to treat all manner of ailments, had been switched off at the close of business the night before. The last treatments were usually completed by 7pm, then everyone went home leaving Monsieur Dupont, the caretaker, to lock up.

Following the sound, Madame Georges entered the majestic Roman spa. The double doors swung silently closed behind her as she made her way towards the pool. She was aware of her feet, still encased in outdoor shoes, making a slapping sound on the tiled floor. Madame Georges immediately noticed that the hoist chair was down and something was bundled up beneath it at the water's edge, but as her spectacles were steamed-up from the damp atmosphere, she couldn't tell what that something was until she was practically on top of it.

"Oh, mon Dieu," she said aloud on realising that what had looked like a bundle of rags, was in fact, a man.

A wave of shock passed through her body; she took off her glasses with shaking hands, cleaned them on the hem of her blouse then stared again. It was definitely a man. His body was still and there was what seemed to be blood gathered in a puddle on the tiles beneath it. Madame Georges did not immediately recognise the person as the head and shoulders were under water. All the staff at 'les thermes' wore pink track-suits and trainers to work, and the guests were usually attired in white, towelling, dressing gowns and blue, rubber, pool shoes. This person was clothed in a dark-coloured suit and had formal shoes on his feet.

Regaining some of her composure, Madame Georges turned and ran back through the double, swing doors towards the office. She used her key to let herself in then immediately pressed the button to sound the alarm. The alarm was a wartime relic, a former air-raid siren, still used to alert people to an emergency. It wailed out over the valley and across the mountains twice. People who would normally have gone back to sleep at the first blast were now fully awake. The queue of chattering shoppers, waiting in line at the 'boulangerie' to buy their baguettes, fell silent, each person straining to listen for approaching emergency vehicles. This double call was used only for the most serious of incidents.

Madame Georges sank into a chair then she picked up the phone and dialled the emergency number to report what she'd discovered.

"Oh, mon Dieu, mon Dieu, a man is dead. I'm sure he is dead. There has been an accident, I think. Assistance, s'il vous plait, please come at once, please help me, I am alone here," she said, when her call was answered. Madame Georges had seen death before many times. The spa attracted the sick and the old searching for cures for various ailments and many of them spent the last days of their lives there, but this was different.

Like a well-oiled machine, everything flowed into action. Before very long the 'pompiers,' who are firemen and trained paramedics, arrived, along with an ambulance and a local practitioner named Doctor Poullet. A crowd began to gather in the street outside. But prior to this whole circus kicking off, I was the first on the scene accompanied by one of my trainee officers. We managed to calm down Madame Georges before securing the area and this is where my story begins.

Deadly Degrees in the Pyrenees

The ghastly murder of a local estate agent reveals unscrupulous business deals which have the whole town talking. Michelle Moliner was not liked, but why would someone want to kill her? The story unfolds, told by Danielle, a single, thirty-something, female cop based in a small French town in the Eastern Pyrenees. Danielle's friends may be in danger and she must discover who the killer is before anyone else is harmed.

Deadly Degrees in the Pyrenees is the 5th book in the Death in the Pyrenees series. It's about life, local events, colourful characters, prejudice and of course death in a small French town

The Unravelling of Thomas Malone

The mutilated corpse of a young prostitute is discovered in a squalid apartment.

Angela Murphy has recently started working as a detective on the mean streets of Glasgow. Just days into the job she's called to attend this grisly murder. She is shocked by the horror of the scene. It's a ghastly sight of blood and despair.

To her boss, Frank Martin, there's something horribly familiar about the scene.

Is this the work of a copycat killer?

Will he strike again?

With limited resources and practically no experience, Angela is desperate to prove herself.

But is her enthusiasm sufficient?

Can she succeed before the killer strikes again?

and here's the first few pages to sample -

Prologue

Thomas Malone remembered very clearly the first time he heard the voice. He was twelve years, five months and three days old. He knew that for a fact because it was January 15th, the same day his mother died.

Thomas lived with his mother Clare in the south side of Glasgow. Their home was a main door apartment in a Victorian terrace. The area had never been grand, but in its time, it housed many incomers to the city. First the Irish, then Jews escaping from Eastern Europe, Italians, Polish, Greeks, Pakistanis, they'd all lived there and built communities. Many of these families became the backbone of Glasgow society. However situations changed and governments came and went and now the same terraces were the dumping ground for economic migrants who had no intention of working legally, but sought an easy existence within the soft welfare state system.

A large number of the properties were in the hands of unscrupulous landlords who were only interested in making money. They didn't care who they housed as long as the rent was paid. So as well as the people fleecing the system, there were also the vulnerable who they exploited. Drug addicts, alcoholics, prostitutes, young single mothers with no support, they were easy pickings for the gangsters. The whole area and the people living within it smacked of decay. It had become a no-go district for decent folk, but to Thomas Malone, it was simply home.

Thomas and his mother moved to their apartment on Westmoreland Street when Clare fell out with her parents. The truth was they really didn't want their wayward daughter living with them any more. They were embarrassed by her friends and hated their drinking and loud music. When Clare became pregnant, it was the last straw. Thomas's grandparents were honest, hard-working, middle-class people who had two other children living at home to consider. So when Clare stormed out one day after yet another row with her mother, they let her go. She waited in a hostel for homeless women for three weeks before she realised they weren't coming to fetch her home and that's when Clare finally grew up and took charge of her life in the only way she knew how.

When Thomas walked home from school along Westmoreland Street, he didn't see that the building's façades were weather worn and blackened with grime from traffic fumes. To outsiders they looked shabby and were reminiscent of a mouth full of rotting teeth, but to Thomas they were familiar and comforting. He didn't notice the litter strewn on the road, the odd discarded shoe, rags snagged on railings, or graffiti declaring 'Joe's a wanker' or 'Mags a slag'. He functioned, each day like the one before, never asking for anything because there was never any money to spare.

He was used to the many 'uncles' who visited his mother. Some were kind to him and gave him money to go to the cinema, but many were drunken and violent. Thomas knew to keep away from them. Sometimes he slept on the stairs in the close rather than in his bed so he could avoid any conflict. He kept a blanket and a cushion in a cardboard box by the door for such occasions. Many a time, when he returned from school, he found his mother with her face battered and bruised crying because the latest 'uncle' had left, never to return. It was far from being an ideal life, but it was all he knew so he had no other expectations.

It was a very cold day and, as he hurried home from school, Thomas's breath froze in great puffs in front of him. He was a skinny boy, small for his age with pixie features common to children of alcoholics. His school shirt and thin blazer did little to keep him warm and he rubbed his bare hands together in an attempt to stop them from hurting. He was glad his school bag was a rucksack because he could sling it over his shoulder to protect his back from the icy wind. As his home drew near his fast walk became a jog, then a run, his lungs were sore from inhaling the cold air, but he didn't care, he would soon be indoors. He would soon be able to open and heat a tin of soup for his dinner and it would fill him up and warm him through. He hoped his mother had remembered to buy some bread to dunk.

As Thomas approached the front door something didn't seem right, he could see that it was slightly ajar and the door was usually kept locked. There was a shoe shaped imprint on the front step, it was red and sticky and Thomas thought it might be blood. There was a red smear on the cream paint of the door frame, he was sure it was blood. Thomas pushed the door and it opened with a creak, there were more bloody prints in the hallway.

Thomas took in a great breath and held it as he made his way down the hall towards the kitchen. He could hear the radio playing softly. Someone was singing 'When I fall in love'. He could smell his mother's perfume it was strong as if the whole bottle had been spilled. The kitchen looked like a bomb had hit it. His mother wasn't much of a housekeeper and the house was usually untidy, but not like this. There was broken crockery and glassware everywhere and the radio, which was plugged in, was hanging by its wire from the socket on the wall, dangling down in front of the kitchen base unit. A large knife was sticking up from the table where it was embedded in the wood. The floor was sticky with blood a great pool of it spread from the sink to the door, in the middle of the pool lay the body of Thomas's mother. She was on her side with one arm outstretched as if she were trying to reach for the door. Her lips were twisted into a grimace, her eyes were wide open and her throat was sliced with a jagged cut from ear to ear. Clare's long brown hair was stuck to her head and to the floor with blood and her cotton housecoat was parted slightly to expose one blood-smeared breast.

Thomas felt his skinny legs give from under him, he sank to his knees and his mother's blood smeared his trousers and shoes. He could hear a terrible sound filling the room, a guttural, animal keening which reached a crescendo into a shrieking howl. Over and over the noise came, filling his ears and his mind with terror. Then he heard the voice in his head.

"It's all right, Son," it said. "Everything will be all right. I'm with you now and I'll help you."

He felt strong arms lift him from the floor and a policeman wrapped him in a blanket.

"Don't be frightened," the voice told him. "Just go with the policeman. Someone else will sort out this mess. It's not your problem. Forget about it."

"Thank you," he mouthed, but no sound came out.

The policeman gathered Thomas in his arms and carried him from the room. It was the last time he ever saw his mother and he cannot remember now how she looked before she was murdered. The voice in his head, the voice that helped him then, remains with him today guiding and instructing him, often bullying, it rules his every thought. Sometimes Thomas gets angry with it but he always obeys it.

The Coming of the Lord

Breaking the Thomas Malone case was an achievement but nothing could prepare DC Angela Murphy or her colleagues for the challenge ahead.

Escaped psychopathic sociopath John Baptiste, is big, powerful and totally out of control. Guided by his perverse religious interpretation of morality, he wreaks havoc.

An under-resourced police department struggles to cope, not only with this new threat, but also the ruthless antics of ganglord Jackie McGeachy.

Pressure mounts along with the body count.

Glasgow has never felt more dangerous.

Never Ever Leave Me

Hi, my name is Elly Grant and I like to kill people. I use a variety of methods. Some I drop from a great height, others I drown, but I've nothing against suffocation, stabbing, poisoning or simply battering a person to death. As long as it grabs my reader's attention, I'm satisfied. I've written several novels and short stories. My series 'Death in the Pyrenees' comprises, 'Palm Trees in the Pyrenees,' 'Grass Grows in the Pyrenees,' 'Red Light in the Pyrenees', 'Dead End in the Pyrenees' and 'Deadly Degrees in the Pyrenees'. They are all set in a small town in France. These novels are published by Author Way Limited. Author Way has also published, 'The Unravelling of Thomas Malone' which is set in Scotland, as well as a collaboration of short stories written with author Zach Abrams titled 'Twists and Turns', and, written together with author Angi Fox, the darkly humourous novel, 'But Billy Can't Fly'. As I live much of my life in a small French town in the Eastern Pyrenees, I get inspiration for my books which are set there, from the way of life and the colourful characters I come across. I don't have to search very hard to find things to write about and living in the most prolific wine producing region in France makes the task so much more delightful. Perhaps you will visit my town one day. Perhaps you will sit near me in a café or return my smile as I walk past you in the street. Perhaps you will hold my interest for a while, and maybe, just maybe, you will be my next victim. But don't concern yourself too much, because, at least for the time being, I always manage to confine my murderous ways to paper. Read books from the 'Death in the Pyrenees' series, enter my small French town and meet some of the people who live there – and die there. Alternatively read about life on some of the toughest streets in Glasgow or for something more varied delve into my short stories.

Death at Presley Park

In the center of a leafy suburb, everyone is having fun until the unthinkable happens. The man walks into the middle of the picnic ground seemingly unnoticed and without warning, opens fire indiscriminately into the startled crowd. People collapse, wounded and dying. Those who can, flee for their lives.

Who is this madman and why is he here? And when stakes are high, who will become a hero and who will abandon their friends?

Elly Grant's Death At Presley Park is a convincing psychological thriller.

But Billy Can't Fly

At over six feet tall, blonde and blue-eyed, Billy looks like an Adonis, but he is simple minded, not the full shilling, one slice less than a sandwich, not quite right in the head. When you meet him you might not notice at first, but after a couple of minutes it becomes apparent. The lights are on but nobody's home. In Billy's mind, he's Superman, a righter of wrongs, a saver of souls and that's where it all goes wrong. He interacts with the people he meets at a bus stop, Jez, a rich public schoolboy, Melanie the office slut, Bella Worthington, the leader of the local W.I. and David, a gay, Jewish teacher. This book moves quickly along as each character tells their part of the tale. Billy's story is darkly funny, poignant and tragic. Full of stereotypical prejudices, it offends on every level, but is difficult to put down.

Released by Elly Grant Together with Zach Abrams

Twists and Turns

With fear, horror, death and despair, these stories will surprise you, scare you and occasionally make you smile. *Twists and Turns* offer the reader thought provoking tales. Whether you have a minute to spare or an hour or more, open *Twists and Turns* for a world full of mystery, murder, revenge and intrigue. A unique collaboration from the authors Elly Grant and Zach Abrams

Here's the index of Twists and Turns -

Table of Contents

A selection of stories by Elly Grant and Zach Abrams ranging in length across flash fiction (under 250 words), short (under 1000 words) medium (under 5000 words) and long (approx. 16,000 words)

- Courting Disaster (medium) by Zach Abrams

- Crash (flash) by Zach Abrams

- Submarine (medium) by Elly Grant

- Dilemma (flash) by Zach Abrams

- Grass is Greener (medium) by Zach Abrams

- Missing (flash) by Elly Grant

- Time to Kill (medium) by Elly Grant

- Fight (flash) by Zach Abrams

- Just Desserts (medium) by Elly Grant

- Interruption (flash) by Zach Abrams

- I've Got Your Number (medium) by Elly Grant

- Rhetoric (flash) by Zach Abrams

- Keep It to Yourself (medium) by Zach Abrams

- Lost, Never to be Found] (medium) by Zach Abrams

- Man of Principal] (flash) by Zach Abrams

- Witness After the Fact] (medium) by Zach Abrams

- Overheated] (flash) by Zach Abrams

- Wedded Blitz] (medium) by Elly Grant

- Taken Care] (flash) by Zach Abrams

- The Others] (short) by Elly Grant

- Waiting for Martha] (long) by Elly Grant

and here's the first few pages to sample -

Waiting for Martha

The 'whoooo aaaaah' accompanied by blood curdling shrieks sent the Campbell brothers screaming down the path. They tore along the street without a backward glance. Martha Davis and her three companions doubled up with laughter. They were all dressed as zombies and, to the naïve eyes of primary school-aged children, they were the real thing.

"Did you see the middle one move?" Alan Edwards asked. "He could be a candidate for the Olympics. He easily left his big brother behind."

"That's because the older one's a lard ass," John Collins replied unkindly. "His bum cheeks wobbled like a jelly. Fat kids shouldn't wear lycra. If the real Superman was that chunky he'd never get off the ground."

"The middle one overtook him because he was trying to help the younger one and was holding his hand," Martha observed. "I'm sure that little fellow pee-ed his pants, he was terrified. He's only about five."

"Yeah, great isn't it?" Fiona Bell added laughing. "I love Halloween, don't you?" she said clapping her gloved hands together with pleasure.

The teenagers had hidden round the corner of Alan's house to jump out at unsuspecting children who came trick or treating. They were all aged fifteen except for John Collins whose birthday had been in June, he was sixteen but looked older. He was a big lad, tall and broad with an athletic build, he looked like a grown-up where the others still looked like children. Fiona Bell was nearly sixteen her birthday was on the fifth of November, Guy Fawkes night, so the group would be celebrating next week with fireworks. She was the spitting image of her mother being of medium height with long blonde hair and a heart shaped pretty face. Alan Edwards's birthday was in January. He was short with straggly black hair and he was a bit of a joker. Martha Davis, the baby of the group, was born in March and was a willowy looking beauty with Titian coloured hair. They were in the same class at school and had a reputation for being cool and edgy. None of them was ever actually caught for their various misdemeanours, but they were often seen running away from trouble. Being teenagers they thought they knew it all and, smoking, drinking, wearing only black and never telling their parents anything, was par for the course. Living in a village meant they didn't have easy access to drugs but the friends made roll-ups using everything from dried orange peel to crushed tree bark and convinced each other it had some psychedelic effect. They'd all been born in the village and had been friends since playgroup. They trusted one another with their worries and secrets and their friendships endured through petty squabbles and jealousies. Although unrelated, they were like a family.

By seven o'clock the procession of 'victims' had all but dried up, the word had got out, it seemed, so Martha and her friends decided to change venue.

"Time to go to church," Alan suggested. "If we hide just inside the gates of the churchyard, we'll get them as they walk by."

"That's a great idea," John added. "They'll think we've risen out of one of the churchyard graves. We'll scare the shit out of the little darlings."

"You lot go ahead and I'll catch you up. I'm going home for a warmer sweater and a quick bite to eat. I've not had my dinner yet and I'm starving. I'll just be about half an hour," Martha assured.

"Why didn't you grab something to eat before you came out? The rest of us did. Now you'll miss out on some of the fun," Fiona said, disappointedly. Martha was her best girl friend and she didn't want to be stuck on her own with the two boys. They could get incredibly silly without Martha. She was the mother figure of the group and she always managed to stop them from going too far.

"Don't worry Fiona, I'll not be long, and you two," she said pointing to the boys, "Behave yourselves."

"Yes Mom," they replied in unison, hanging their heads and pulling comical faces.

"See what I have to put up with when your not there, anyone would think they were two years old."

Martha stared at her three friends, her face had a serious expression and for a moment it looked as if she might cry. "I love you guys," she said. "I'll be as quick as I can."

"Are you okay?" Fiona asked. "You look a bit upset."

"I'm fine, really fine. My eyes are just watering with the cold. It's freezing out here."

Martha gave each of them a hug and off she raced towards her home. The others quickly made their way to the church and positioned themselves behind one of the large wrought iron gates. The gates hadn't been closed for over fifty years and ivy grew thickly round them affording the teenagers cover. For the next forty minutes they had a ball scaring adults and children alike until one of their teachers, Mr Johnston, came along. As the three friends jumped out shrieking he clutched his heart and fell to the ground. They thought they'd killed him. They were kneeling on the ground beside him each trying to decide how to do CPR when he suddenly sat up and shouted "Got ya." The tables were well and truly turned and they nearly jumped out of their skins.

"It's not so funny when you're on the receiving end is it?" he said rising to his feet. "Haven't you got homes to go to? And where's the fourth one? Where's your friend, Martha?"

"She went home for some food," Fiona said. "She should have been back by now."

"I think you should all run along and find her. You've done enough damage here for one night?"

Mr Johnston brushed himself down and walked away. After their shock the three friends had indeed had enough.

"Martha should have been here ages ago," Alan said. "I'm getting cold now. Let's go to her house and see what's keeping her."

"Good idea," John agreed.

"But what if she's on her way and we miss her?" Fiona protested.

"Come on," Alan said pulling her arm. "I'm not waiting any longer and you can't stay here on your own. A real zombie might leap out of a grave and get you. If Martha arrives and we're gone she'll go home and she'll find us there."

"I suppose you're right," Fiona conceded.

"I'm always right," Alan said smugly. "Come on let's get going before my ears fall off with the cold."

The three friends headed along the street towards Martha's home. They were damp and tired and they hoped that Helen Davis, Martha's mum, had hot soup for them. She always had soup on the stove in winter and she fed the three of them as if they were her family.

"I hope Mrs Davis has pumpkin soup, it's my favourite," John said,

"Yeah, the chilli she puts in it really gives it a kick," Alan agreed.

"Aren't either of you just a teensy bit worried about Martha? She's been gone for over an hour now and she's never usually late," Fiona said. "Get a move on, you two. I want to make sure she's all right."

When they reached Martha's house and rang the bell they were surprised when her Dad, Michael, answered instead of her.

"Well, well, what have we here?" he asked laughing at their attire. "Is Martha hiding? Where is she?"

"She left us over an hour ago to come home for food," Fiona said. "We thought she was still here. When did she leave the house?"

"Martha hasn't been home," her father replied. "If this is some sort of Halloween joke, it's not funny." He stared at the teenagers. "The joke's over. Where's Martha?"

A chill ran through each of the friends and Fiona's eyes welled with tears. "We don't know," she said helplessly. "If she didn't come home then she's been gone for over an hour. Something might have happened to her, maybe she's fallen. We'd better go back and look for her."

"Wait for me. I'm coming with you," Mr Davis replied. "I'll just go and tell Martha's mum what's happening."

After a couple of minutes, Michael Davis returned and Helen was with him. When she saw the state Fiona was in, Helen put her arm round the crying girl's shoulders and tried to reassure her. "Don't worry, Pet, we'll find her," she said. "She won't have gone far. She probably stopped to chat to someone and lost track of the time."

"We'll split into three groups," Michael Davis said. "Alan and John, you take the street leading to the church. Helen and Fiona, you walk towards the primary school and I'll take the road that goes round the outside of the village. We'll meet back here in half an hour. No, better make it forty-five minutes," he said looking at his watch.

The boys looked uncomfortably at Fiona; they would have much rather stayed together but they had no choice. Mr Davis had taken control and, as he was an adult and a teacher, they felt they should do what he said. Besides, the sooner they found Martha the sooner they could go home, assuming of course that they did find Martha.

They searched the whole village knocking on several doors as they went. The group met up after the arranged forty-five minutes then searched again. By ten o'clock there was nowhere left to look for her. The next day was a school day and the three teenagers had now reached their curfew, but they were reluctant to go home with Martha still missing. Michael Davis was grim faced. Helen was beginning to panic.

About the Author

Hi, my name is Elly Grant and I like to kill people. I use a variety of methods. Some I drop from a great height, others I drown, but I've nothing against suffocation, poisoning or simply battering a person to death. As long as it grabs my reader's attention, I'm satisfied.

I've written several novels and short stories. My first novel, 'Palm Trees in the Pyrenees' is set in a small town in France. It is published by Author Way Limited. Author Way has already published the next three novels in the series, 'Grass Grows in the Pyrenees,' 'Red Light in the Pyrenees' and 'Dead End in the Pyrenees' as well as a collaboration of short stories called 'Twists and Turns'.

As I live in a small French town in the Eastern Pyrenees, I get inspiration from the way of life and the colourful characters I come across. I don't have to search very hard to find things to write about and living in the most prolific wine producing region in France makes the task so much more delightful.

When I first arrived in this region I was lulled by the gentle pace of life, the friendliness of the people and the simple charm of the place. But dig below the surface and, like people and places the world over, the truth begins to emerge. Petty squabbles, prejudice, jealousy and greed are all there waiting to be discovered. Oh, and what joy in that discovery. So, as I sit in a café, or stroll by the riverside, or walk high into the mountains in the sunshine I greet everyone I meet with a smile and a 'Bonjour' and, being a friendly place, they return the greeting. I people watch as I sip my wine or when I go to buy my baguette. I discover quirkiness and quaintness around every corner. I try to imagine whether the subjects of my scrutiny are nice or nasty and, once I've decided, some of those unsuspecting people, a very select few, I kill.

Perhaps you will visit my town one day. Perhaps you will sit near me in a café or return my smile as I walk past you in the street. Perhaps you will hold my interest for a while, and maybe, just maybe, you will be my next victim. But don't concern yourself too much, because, at least for the time being, I always manage to confine my murderous ways to paper.

Read books from the 'Death in the Pyrenees' series, enter my small French town and meet some of the people who live there —– and die there.

To contact the author ellygrant@authorway.net